Yukon Madness

SELECTED FICTION WORKS BY L. RON HUBBARD

FANTASY

The Case of the Friendly Corpse

Death's Deputy

Fear

The Ghoul

The Indigestible Triton

Slaves of Sleep & The Masters of Sleep

Typewriter in the Sky

The Ultimate Adventure

SCIENCE FICTION

Battlefield Earth

The Conquest of Space

The End Is Not Yet

Final Blackout

The Kilkenny Cats

The Kingslayer

The Mission Earth Dekalogy*

Ole Doc Methuselah

To the Stars

ADVENTURE

The Hell Job series

WESTERN

Buckskin Brigades

Empty Saddles

Guns of Mark Jardine

Hot Lead Payoff

A full list of L. Ron Hubbard's
novellas and short stories is provided at the back.

*Dekalogy—a group of ten volumes

L. RON
HUBBARD

Yukon
Madness

Published by
Galaxy Press, LLC
7051 Hollywood Boulevard, Suite 200
Hollywood, CA 90028

Printed in the United States of America.

ISBN-10 1-59212-317-1
ISBN-13 978-1-59212-317-9

Library of Congress Control Number: 2007903545

Contents

Stories from Pulp Fiction's Golden Age

A ND it *was* a golden age.
The 1930s and 1940s were a vibrant, seminal time for a gigantic audience of eager readers, probably the largest per capita audience of readers in American history. The magazine racks were chock-full of publications with ragged trims, garish cover art, cheap brown pulp paper, low cover prices—and the most excitement you could hold in your hands.

"Pulp" magazines, named for their rough-cut, pulpwood paper, were a vehicle for more amazing tales than Scheherazade could have told in a million and one nights. Set apart from higher-class "slick" magazines, printed on fancy glossy paper with quality artwork and superior production values, the pulps were for the "rest of us," adventure story after adventure story for people who liked to *read*. Pulp fiction authors were no-holds-barred entertainers—real storytellers. They were more interested in a thrilling plot twist, a horrific villain or a white-knuckle adventure than they were in lavish prose or convoluted metaphors.

The sheer volume of tales released during this wondrous golden age remains unmatched in any other period of literary history—hundreds of thousands of published stories in over nine hundred different magazines. Some titles lasted only an issue or two; many magazines succumbed to paper shortages during World War II, while others endured for decades yet. Pulp fiction remains as a treasure trove of stories you can read, stories you can love, stories you can remember. The stories were driven by plot and character, with grand heroes, terrible villains, beautiful damsels (often in distress), diabolical plots, amazing places, breathless romances. The readers wanted to be taken beyond the mundane, to live adventures far removed from their ordinary lives—and the pulps rarely failed to deliver.

In that regard, pulp fiction stands in the tradition of all memorable literature. For as history has shown, good stories are much more than fancy prose. William Shakespeare, Charles Dickens, Jules Verne, Alexandre Dumas—many of the greatest literary figures wrote their fiction for the readers, not simply literary colleagues and academic admirers. And writers for pulp magazines were no exception. These publications reached an audience that dwarfed the circulations of today's short story magazines. Issues of the pulps were scooped up and read by over thirty million avid readers each month.

Because pulp fiction writers were often paid no more than a cent a word, they had to become prolific or starve. They also had to write aggressively. As Richard Kyle, publisher and editor of *Argosy*, the first and most long-lived of the pulps, so pointedly explained: "The pulp magazine writers, the best of them, worked for markets that did not write for critics or attempt to satisfy timid advertisers. Not having to answer to anyone other than their readers, they wrote about human beings on the edges of the unknown, in those new lands the future would explore. They wrote for what we would become, not for what we had already been."

Some of the more lasting names that graced the pulps include H. P. Lovecraft, Edgar Rice Burroughs, Robert E. Howard, Max Brand, Louis L'Amour, Elmore Leonard, Dashiell Hammett, Raymond Chandler, Erle Stanley Gardner, John D. MacDonald, Ray Bradbury, Isaac Asimov, Robert Heinlein—and, of course, L. Ron Hubbard.

In a word, he was among the most prolific and popular writers of the era. He was also the most enduring—hence this series—and certainly among the most legendary. It all began only months after he first tried his hand at fiction, with L. Ron Hubbard tales appearing in *Thrilling Adventures*, *Argosy*, *Five-Novels Monthly*, *Detective Fiction Weekly*, *Top-Notch*, *Texas Ranger*, *War Birds*, *Western Stories*, even *Romantic Range*. He could write on any subject, in any genre, from jungle explorers to deep-sea divers, from G-men and gangsters, cowboys and flying aces to mountain climbers, hard-boiled detectives and spies. But he really began to shine when he turned his talent to science fiction and fantasy of which he authored nearly fifty novels or novelettes to forever change the shape of those genres.

Following in the tradition of such famed authors as Herman Melville, Mark Twain, Jack London and Ernest Hemingway, Ron Hubbard actually lived adventures that his own characters would have admired—as an ethnologist among primitive tribes, as prospector and engineer in hostile climes, as a captain of vessels on four oceans. He even wrote a series of articles for *Argosy*, called "Hell Job," in which he lived and told of the most dangerous professions a man could put his hand to.

Finally, and just for good measure, he was also an accomplished photographer, artist, filmmaker, musician and educator. But he was first and foremost a *writer*, and that's the L. Ron Hubbard we come to know through the pages of this volume.

This library of Stories from the Golden Age presents the best of L. Ron Hubbard's fiction from the heyday of storytelling, the Golden Age of the pulp magazines. In these eighty volumes, readers are treated to a full banquet of 153 stories, a kaleidoscope of tales representing every imaginable genre: science fiction, fantasy, western, mystery, thriller, horror, even romance—action of all kinds and in all places.

Because the pulps themselves were printed on such inexpensive paper with high acid content, issues were not meant to endure. As the years go by, the original issues of every pulp from *Argosy* through *Zeppelin Stories* continue crumbling into brittle, brown dust. This library preserves the L. Ron Hubbard tales from that era, presented with a distinctive look that brings back the nostalgic flavor of those times.

L. Ron Hubbard's Stories from the Golden Age has something for every taste, every reader. These tales will return you to a time when fiction was good clean entertainment and the most fun a kid could have on a rainy afternoon or the best thing an adult could enjoy after a long day at work.

Pick up a volume, and remember what reading is supposed to be all about. Remember curling up with a *great story*.

—Kevin J. Anderson

KEVIN J. ANDERSON *is the author of more than ninety critically acclaimed works of speculative fiction, including The Saga of Seven Suns, the continuation of the Dune Chronicles with Brian Herbert, and his* New York Times *bestselling novelization of L. Ron Hubbard's* Ai! Pedrito!

Yukon Madness

Yukon Madness

ITAUK THE MADMAN, stalking across the bitter
wastes, squinting with slanted eyes over the backs of his
twelve-wolf team, stared into the blackness toward the
snarling flares of red and green and white which shot into the
indigo winter sky—the aurora borealis. Itauk the Madman,
a horror in the raw north of Hudson Bay, spreading death
with sharp steel and throwing the shattered bodies of men
to his slavering team.

Twelve wolves as black as the winter sky, glittering teeth
as sharp as the white ice which jutted through the dry snow,
mouths as red-flecked as the borealis, tugged at the sledge
traces. And Itauk laughed—a piercing, grating laughter which
splintered the great silence.

Tommy McKenna heard the laugh, though it was far away.
And Tommy McKenna shuddered under his red coat and
sealskin parka. He could see nothing, but he heard. The cold
barrel of the Lee-Enfield was hard under his tight fingers.
His eyes—gray eyes as cold as arctic ice—closed to lines.

That was Itauk. The sound came far through the ebon
chill. That was Itauk and Billy Simmons was back at camp
alone, sleeping. Or was he sleeping still? Had Itauk struck
again in the Yukon Territory?

Tommy McKenna raised his snowshoes and struck out

in a rapid lope for camp. He had forgotten the bear tracks he had seen earlier in the day. He had forgotten that he and Simmons were almost out of food. He remembered only his charge to "get his man."

"Get Itauk!" the lieutenant had ordered at Post Ledoux. It had sent McKenna and Simmons on a five-hundred-mile trek through blackness, through acid cold, across uncharted seas of snow.

And now Itauk's laugh out of the ebon cold. Tommy McKenna's snowshoes rapped the dry crust in a steady tempo. His lean, weathered face—handsome before it had been too long exposed to screaming winds and silent mountains of white—was almost buried in the fur hood. It was fifty-five below and a man's breath froze in his nostrils and stayed there, freezing his lungs.

He came within a hundred yards of the camp and stopped. He called out, his voice clear as a trumpet, "Simmons!"

No answer. Heavy, throbbing silence. The flare and flash of the northern lights as they shot spitefully up at the stars. A wolf howled out in the cold alone, dismal and quavering. Answering the call.

Calling "Simmons!" again, he listened intently.

Tommy McKenna threw off the safety of the Enfield. His mittens were clumsy but he dared not take them off. His hands would freeze to the barrel of his gun.

"Simmons!"

Uncertain now. Knowledge as icy as the half-year night told Tommy McKenna that he would never again hear Simmons' voice. With that sixth or perhaps seventh sense born in men who stand eye to eye with danger and the raw North, Tommy McKenna already understood.

He advanced slowly. The fire was a red glow against the blue darkness. The flame had died down. A shadow lay against it, a shadow queerly limp and empty.

Tommy McKenna stared at the patch of scarlet cloth. A bright warm stain was growing in the dry snow, spreading out slowly and steadily.

Simmons' face had been torn away as though by claws. Nothing remained but the broken, red-shredded skull. Tufts of his parka lay black against the white. Blood was scattered far.

Tommy McKenna's voice was stiff, unreal. "He . . . turned his wolves . . . to feast . . ."

Anger blocked out the body, blacked the northern lights. Tommy's hands shook with rage. He looked north and his eyes were chill.

The unwritten law of the Mounties: Swift death to those who would kill one of us.

Itauk would die. With either bullets or steel or bare hands. No trial for Itauk now. He had committed the unforgivable crime, punishable by instant death on sight. He had killed Simmons of the Royal Canadian Mounted Police. No wooden gallows in the Yukon Territory headquarters, with a priest to see Itauk through death's door; it had to come when—and as soon as death could!

Tommy McKenna looked back at the fire. The torn fur and scattered bones of the sledge dogs told a swift story. Tommy knew that he was on foot, that he would have to live from kill to kill—unless he met Itauk.

The garish flame of the northern lights showed up the trail. The large pads of Itauk's wolves had left their plain print upon the snow, and over the pads was the print of a *kamik*-covered foot. That was Itauk.

Picking up a bundle of supplies from the ruin of their outfit, Tommy struck out. His snowshoes rasped over the dry cold surface and the weight of the Enfield was hard against his arm. No time to bury Simmons now. The pause might lose him his quarry.

Slogging through the never-ending night, Tommy heard the sounds of the North: the crackle of ice under terrific stress; the moan of sharp wind across the great reaches; the shivering hunting cry of the wolf.

For hours the trail was straight, leading into the very heart of the borealis. Itauk the Madman was traveling fast and far, lengthening the road which was milestoned with blood.

Tommy's breath was ice on his lips and his lungs burned from exertion and freezing air. The Enfield grew heavier. The revolver under the parka banged with steady monotony against his thigh.

His squinted eyes did not leave the trail. The sound of his snowshoes was like the staccato flicking of sandpaper across a drumhead.

He stopped, still looking down, his practiced glance reading the story.

Someone had intercepted Itauk's trail. The sledge had stopped. Then a pair of shoes led off at an angle, traveling west.

It seemed to Tommy that the second prints were lighter,

but he did not think that Itauk would desert his team—nor did Tommy think that any man in the North could drive the twelve wolves except Itauk.

He followed the sledge runners again, quickening his pace. The wind was stronger, sending whirlwinds of dry snow rocketing up toward the black sky.

Two months until morning. A hundred miles to the first Mountie post. Tommy felt alone and cold and weary. But his eyes held the trail.

The northern lights flared higher and higher until they covered the entire dome of the sky. The world stood out stark and bitter like the ocean seen through a lightning flash. Far ahead against the rim, Tommy saw a string of dots.

As he quickened his pace, he thought that perhaps he would have a showdown now, even though Itauk, riding his runners, would be fresh.

Seconds were ticked away by the rasping shoes. Another flare of the lights. A hundred yards in front of him, Tommy beheld the team.

But the revelation was mutual. The sledge stopped. Tommy slowed up, watchful, walking like a cat. The dim shadow before him might rush him. The Enfield was balanced, safety off.

Still the shadow did not move. Less than twenty feet away, the wolves growled low in their throats.

Tommy, moving an inch at a time, closed the gap. The shadow was immobile. A white blur showed in the parka hood.

"Itauk," said Tommy McKenna, "drop your gun!" His voice

was quiet, steady, more than assured, but an instant later the tone had changed: "My God!"

The shadow crumpled abruptly, pitching headfirst into the trail. Tommy, holding his rifle in one hand, caught at the shoulder.

A vibrant voice answered him, hesitant with sobs, "Don't . . . don't kill me!"

It was a girl!

Her face was not that of an ordinary Eskimo woman. It was finer, more delicate. Nor were the eyes slanted. Her figure was slight and although it was almost hidden under the bulk of her furs, Tommy caught an impression of a slender body, small hands, a high, firm breast.

He lifted her up, a little angry now. "Where is Itauk?"

"Who is Itauk?"

"Where is the man you met down this trail?"

She shook her head and averted her eyes. "I know no Itauk."

Tommy's mouth went hard. "I am McKenna of the Royal Mounted."

"But . . . but I have done nothing."

Tommy experienced a sudden hunch that this girl was not an ally of the Madman, that she was innocent of any complicity in his crimes. But if that were so, then why had she attempted to help Itauk out by throwing a Mountie off the trail? Or had Itauk been unaware of pursuit?

"Where is your village?" demanded Tommy. "Your igloo?"

"An . . . an hour's travel from here. I have done nothing. Do not arrest me." She was regaining her pride now. Something of defiance had crept into her tone. She held her head high and looked at him.

"Take me there," ordered Tommy.

She drew back the whip. It sizzled and cracked beside the right ear of the lead wolf. He sprang up and into the traces. The others lunged forward.

Riding the runners, the girl drove the team ahead. Tommy fell in beside her, trotting to keep pace with the sledge. In the fitful glare, he could see her high cheekbones and intelligent forehead. He did not need a second look to tell him that she was beautiful—and dangerous.

The skin *igdlut,* banked with snow and ice to keep the warmth within, were built in a depression which afforded some protection from the raking wind. Part of the icy walls had been broken away. A few people, black dots against the white, were visible. Trails of wind-shredded white smoke lifted themselves out of the huts.

A chorus of voices greeted the two and were then instantly still. Surprise showed on the faces of the men. The girl paid them no attention. She drove up before the low entrance of an *igdlu* and called out.

An old man ducked through the entrance and blinked at her, his flat face without expression.

"Tie up these wolves against the coming of The Stranger," she ordered, tossing him the whip and dropping to her knees to crawl through the opening. Tommy followed, dragging the gun by its muzzle.

In the interior of the hut it was warm. Furs covered the

couches along the sides and a cooking pot simmered cheerfully upon the fire. She explained that part of the icy walls had been taken out recently for repairs, and he noticed the "quarried" blocks of ice and cured skins in readiness.

The girl paid Tommy no attention. She stripped off her parka and sealskin *kamiks* and laid them upon a couch. She undressed, straightened her shirt—made of dearly bought cloth—and patted her soft skin skirt until it lay smoothly along her thighs. Putting on a pair of lighter boots and pulling another fur coat around her, she held her hands to the fire, looking sideways at Tommy.

"My name," she said, "is Kaja. This is my home. You are free to eat of my food." Her half-white features lit up with a smile.

Tommy nodded. He pulled off his fur coat and his undercap and threw them down beside hers. She stared at him a moment, slightly dazzled by his scarlet coat and blazing buttons. Then her eyes fell to the holstered revolver and cartridge belt. A rawhide thong around his neck was attached to the butt of the revolver.

"You called him The Stranger. Why?" Tommy watched her closely, quizzically, and at the same time admiring her stunningly beautiful body.

"Because," she paused and laughed, "because he is a stranger. He came to us days ago. He is strong, a mighty hunter, a good provider."

"Why did you take his sledge for him?"

"Because . . . because he said . . . he said that a man was following him, and that the man would not kill a woman."

"Does that mean you intend to marry The Stranger?"

"Why shouldn't I marry him? He is strong, a good provider. Since my brothers were crushed in the ice, I have no one here and I find the men of the tribe weak. No one!"

Outside one of Itauk's sledge wolves howled in hunger. The wind moaned over the hut. Tommy shivered and stepped closer to the fire. He had not shivered from fear. He was used to this untamed country. He had not shivered because of the impending clash with Itauk.

He had shivered because he had been so long away from laughter. This girl—something like an electric current seemed to pass between them. He steadied himself.

"Then you know nothing of The Stranger?"

"No," replied Kaja. "Nothing except that he is strong, a good hunter, rich in goods. I am tired of being alone."

She seemed to lean closer to him. Tommy clenched his hands behind his back. Abruptly he swept her close to him.

Her eyes were large, afraid, but her lips were trembling. She raised her mouth to his. He kissed her, and saw that her eyes were open. Her lips were warm and sweet. Her hands under his shoulders tightened.

Tommy heard the voices outside, heard the crunch of snowshoes. And still he could not let her go. He felt a jerk at his side. Something hard stabbed him above his belt.

The girl backed away, her eyes blazing. She had his gun! In that instant, Tommy started to snatch her wrist, but he knew before he could move that she would shoot.

A brittle voice rapped behind Tommy. "So. It is the Mountie."

11

Tommy turned. Itauk was standing just behind him. Itauk's stringy black hair came down in straight vicious lines on either side of his face. Itauk's eyes were glittering with an insane fire. Itauk's great hands clutched the barrel and stock of Simmons' rifle.

The girl backed away, mouth tight with sudden fear. It was obvious that she had never seen Itauk that way, had never seen the killer light distort a man's face.

Itauk's ugly mouth did not move as he spoke. "Kaja! Give me his gun."

"No, Itauk! No!" She pulled the fur parka closer around her body, her breasts visibly rising and falling with the emotion of the moment.

Itauk's voice was lower, threatening. "Give me that gun."

Coolly she backed further away from him. Itauk centered the Enfield muzzle on Tommy's chest and stepped after her. His hand shot out and clutched her wrist. She struggled to get free.

With a jerk he secured the revolver. The back of his hand swept down, cracking against her cheek. She fell into a sobbing huddle on the couch.

Tommy knew that he could do nothing against Itauk. In the moment Itauk was turned away from him, Tommy stripped off his cartridge belt and threw it toward the cooking pot.

Itauk whirled, laughing. "I will do away with her, later. She has not yet given me what I want, and what I want I take. First, I will do away with you."

Tommy looked at the girl. Her shirt was torn down one

shoulder, and through the rent her creamy skin shone like
satin. Her cheek was streaked with the mark of Itauk's blow.

"Go outside," ordered Itauk.

Tommy stooped to pick up his parka but Itauk stopped him.

"You won't need that, Mountie. You won't need anything
in a very little while."

Tommy ducked and went out. The cold wind stabbed
through his scarlet coat. Fifty-five below, too cold to snow.

The people of the village came hesitantly out of their huts.
They failed to understand the reason, but when they saw
Itauk's face they understood Itauk—understood that he was
a killer.

They had some faint idea that this was a Mountie and that
Itauk was wanted by the law. But they could not understand
Itauk's rage. Had they been other than Eskimos they would
have thought instantly that Itauk was revenging himself upon
the Mountie for the taking of Itauk's woman-to-be. But
neither they nor Itauk could consider this a crime.

Behind the hut Tommy saw Itauk's wolves lying in the
snow. They were watching Itauk with red-shot eyes.

Beside an ice pinnacle, Itauk ordered Tommy to stand.
Itauk shifted the Enfield and pulled a bundle of thongs from
under his shirt.

"If you were clever," said Itauk, smiling with his ugly mouth
but not his eyes, "you would prefer the gun to what I have to
offer you. I am going to lash you there and then I am going
to throw buckets of water against your legs until you are a
block of ice from your toes to your waist."

"And then?" said Tommy, seemingly unperturbed.

"And then I'm going to turn my wolves loose on you to finish you off. They haven't been fed since your red-coated friend was so obliging to them."

Tommy stiffened. Itauk saw the warning in the Mountie's face. Itauk slammed the rifle barrel into Tommy's chest, driving him back against the pillar of ice.

Working with swift hands, Itauk bound the Mountie's wrists, passing the thongs across the scarlet coat and behind the column.

Itauk turned to the Eskimos. "I want water! Buckets of water, quick!"

They scurried before the lash of his words. Women came fearfully forth, not daring to disobey, and placed copper cooking pots at Itauk's feet. The instant the wind struck them, the surface was frozen. Itauk poured out a cupful at Tommy's feet, laughing. The stream froze upright, like a sword blade sticking out of the snow.

Tommy, half-frozen from the wind, dizzy from the blow in the chest, glanced down the hill before them, through the darkness toward the borealis.

No help would come now. But someday Itauk would die under Mountie guns. At least, thought Tommy, he would be avenged.

Kaja came forth from her hut, walking swiftly toward the crowd. Her face was streaked with tears but rage burned there. Her clenched hands were empty. People fell away to let her pass through.

She came up to Itauk, touching his shoulder. He whirled on her. "What do you want now, Kaja?"

"Do not do this thing." She was not begging. Her face was held high to his. Her gaze was level.

"And why not? Is it possible that you would like to die with this man? My dogs, Kaja, are very hungry."

Politely she disregarded the threat. "This man is a man and you are a madman. You must go from our village. My men will not let you do this. And the police will hang you if they catch you, Itauk."

Itauk laughed. His glance swept around the circle of faces behind him. The hunters turned away their heads, ashamed. Itauk's laugh reached a high pitch and then stopped. Snatching Kaja's shoulder he jerked her close to him.

"You think I would listen to women? You do not know who I am, Kaja. You do not know that the man who will soon be your mate is Itauk, the Madman."

The circle backed swiftly. The women ran to their huts. The men stood by, held by curiosity although their wits told them to go.

Itauk shook Kaja like a wolf shakes a rabbit. He threw her away from him and whirled on Tommy. Snatching up the first bucket, Itauk started to throw the stream against the Mountie's legs.

A shot rapped through the great silence. Itauk dropped the water and spun about. Another shot followed and then the hammering of bullets racketed like machine-gun fire. Itauk, face gray with fear, ran in a short circle, staring into

15

the darkness. But he could see no flashes which would place the rifles. He could see no charging men.

Bewildered, he snatched up the Enfield and started in the direction of the fire.

Tommy strained against the thongs. "Kaja!" he cried.

She came swiftly to him. Reaching inside her shirt she pulled forth a short skinning knife and began to cut the bonds.

"I . . . I am sorry," she said, not pausing in her work. "I did not know. I am a traitor. With your kiss still on my mouth I delivered you to Itauk the Madman. Can you ever forget that?"

"Of course I can."

The shots had ceased. Itauk strode through the cluster of huts, raging. Tommy stepped away from the pinnacle of ice, flexing his cold-stiffened arms.

"Quick," said Kaja, "he will come back and you are unarmed. Run out across the plain and hide in the ice. I will find you and—"

"If you could find me, so could Itauk."

Itauk entered Kaja's hut and Tommy stepped behind the ice pillar, out of sight. In a moment Itauk again came into view. Itauk was carrying a cartridge belt which still smoldered. He had dragged it from Kaja's fire.

Looking toward the pinnacle, Itauk uttered a roar of anger. He could see Kaja and he ran toward her, holding the rifle up, ready to shoot. His eyes were shot with red flame like those of a wolf.

Kaja ran past the ice pillar and across the open stretch. Itauk, bellowing, sprinted after her, his black stringy hair standing out behind his head.

16

Tommy crouched in the protection of the hummock and waited. He heard Itauk coming closer and tensed. In an instant Itauk would pass beside the pillar and then . . .

Itauk's arms came into view, then his face. Tommy leaped forward and—missed!

Itauk backed away. He raised the Enfield. The shot was hasty. It snapped as it passed over Tommy's head. Tommy lunged in under the gun.

The Enfield went across the snow, spinning, smoke still spewing from its muzzle. Itauk's hands tugged at the knife in his belt.

Tommy slammed a blow into the greasy face. The knife shimmered as it came away from Itauk's belt. Itauk's hand snapped down like a pile driver. It missed Tommy's face by less than an inch. He tried to seize the wrist and the knife.

Itauk screamed as he felt himself rocked back by another blow. Once more he tried to bring the knife up. Tommy kicked at Itauk's heels and Itauk went down, dragging the Mountie with him.

Parka and scarlet coat blurred in the flurry of snow. Kaja came up, seizing the Enfield, standing back, waiting for a chance to shoot. She saw the blade rise and fall twice. The second time it was red and dripping.

Tommy sagged, his face in the dry white crust. Itauk, roaring triumphantly, leaped up to sink the knife one final time. Tommy rolled. His hands shot out and caught at Itauk's throat.

Itauk cried out. Trying to wriggle free he forgot about the knife. Itauk was conscious only of two thumbs burrowing into his windpipe.

17

She saw the blade rise and fall twice.
The second time it was red and dripping.

They began to roll down the hill, over and over, locked together. Kaja saw the knife go up and come down again. She heard Tommy's startled gasp of surprise.

Itauk, fighting off Tommy's hands, dropped the knife and thrust his palm against the Mountie's chin.

From the region of the huts came an expectant whine which became louder and sharper. The keen noses of the wolves had caught the scent of blood. They were standing up in their traces, gnawing at their confining thongs.

For seconds, Itauk and Tommy remained quiet, exhausted. By straining his head back, Itauk was able to keep the thumbs from sinking deep but his breath came in hoarse rattles.

Tommy, aware only of the terrific pain in his back, had enough presence to retain his hold. Then, through the darkness he heard that swelling whine, heard the heart-freezing expectancy of it. Itauk's wolves were trying to get loose, trying to get down to the fighting men.

That hot, salty stench of blood!

Kaja came slowly down the hill, afraid of her marksmanship, not quite able to bring herself to the task of killing Itauk. She, too, heard that whine and she knew that it would only be a matter of seconds before the black gray horde swept down upon the fighters. She could not hope to hit the wolves, to keep them off.

Down the hillside ran a frozen trail of red, ending with the two at the bottom. Kaja avoided it, moving fearfully, fighting against her impulse to run before the wolves came.

Tommy moved his head from side to side. Itauk's palm

against his chin was slipping. Tommy pressed his thumbs deeper. He could hear that horrible rasping breath above him, knew that the thumbs were doing it.

Suddenly Itauk tore loose. He rolled swiftly to one side. The knife gleamed in the starlight. He snatched at it.

Tommy lunged. Once more his hands fastened on Itauk's throat. The thumbs went deeper and deeper. Itauk tried to sink the blade in Tommy's chest.

An untapped reservoir of strength surged through the Mountie. A savage power coursed down his arms into his hands. His thumbs sank in and seemed to meet his fingers.

He heard Itauk's shriek, heard the swift rush of pads across the snow, heard the snarl of wolves coming down toward them.

Kaja darted to Tommy. She looked up at the shadows sweeping in upon them and then tried to drag Tommy's hands away from the other's throat.

Working with a sob of despair welling up in her breast, she pried away Tommy's fingers.

Snatching Tommy's arms she dragged him swiftly away. The wolves lunged in. The Enfield rapped and a shadow crumpled. The pack swerved away from the flame.

The team leader whirled in his tracks. Suddenly he fell upon Itauk. Wolves closed in, blanketed the body, snarling at each other. The rip of tearing cloth was loud.

Men from the village ran down the hill to Kaja. They knew now that Itauk was dead and the fear of Itauk was far greater than the fear of wolves. They picked up Kaja and Tommy and bore them to the village.

Behind them they could still hear that ripping sound—but not from cloth.

Several hours later, Tommy lifted himself on one elbow, surprised to discover that his wounds did not hurt him. He was once more in the hut of Kaja, lying upon a skin couch covered with furs.

His scarlet coat was carefully folded across the room and his revolver had been restored to the somewhat-charred holster.

Kaja was sitting by the fire, silently looking at him.

"Thanks," said Tommy, simply.

"I owed you more than that," she replied.

Tommy tried to swing down his feet but she held up her hand. "Please don't. Though the knife wounds are not deep, it will take them weeks to fully heal. You must lie down."

Resignedly he sank back. "Weeks, is it? And then the spring breakup will come and I won't be able to get through until summer. It will be months."

She smiled, "I knew that . . . and I am . . ."

He raised himself again, smiling. She shook her head and sat down by his side, stroking his cheek. "You wouldn't take me back with you, nor would you live here with us. We're far apart, yet so close."

"I know," said Tommy. "I . . . please don't touch me. Not like that. Because it . . ."

She smiled. "I know what you are thinking. That you would not want to go away and leave me here if . . ."

"Yes," he said in a quiet voice.

"But that needn't make any difference. You will be here

21

months and after that you may go, forgetting me forever, dearest."

He reached up and dragged her down to him. She pulled herself up. "But your wounds!" she cried.

"Wounds?" said Tommy, his voice dramatically tense. "What wounds? To hell with the wounds."

His hands were behind her shoulders, pulling her down again.

The Cossack

Part One: Sex Lure

COBBLESTONES rang with the cleaving of iron-shod hoofs; the jingle of spur and saber chain mingled with the creak of leather. On the balcony above the colorful courtyard, a stately woman gazed down upon the upturned faces of her cavalry.

At the fore of the red-and-gold picture, his horse's nostrils breathing smokelike steam, his face brown, his hair blondly creeping from under the military primness of his cap, young Lieutenant Mertz Komroff let a bright tongue of Russian sunshine leap from his saber as he saluted.

"Your Highness!" His voice crackled. "Your orders have been carried out and the village lies in ruins. The punitive expedition has been successful and I have lost but two men. I await your pleasure." The saber leaped up in a brief gesture and came again to rest by his shoulder.

Horses shifted nervous, tired feet, curb bits jingled, the morning sun of spring strove to warm the chilled air. Her Highness, the Duchess of Novgrod, stood very still and let her eyes play over the young face below her. A trooper in the far end of the court nudged his fellow and smiled knowingly.

Mertz Komroff shifted his gaze uneasily and jerked at his reins. His horse reared and pawed the air.

"Very good, Lieutenant." Her voice drifted down; softly

sensual, effortless and assured. "You are having dinner with me this evening."

Komroff's horse reared again, and as its forefeet clove the air, the saber came up again in salute, the blade flickering before the troubled expression which had come into his blue gray eyes.

In a thunder of noise and color, the cavalcade wheeled, flashed through the courtyard gates and disappeared beyond the tall iron gates of the barracks.

Her Highness lifted her thin eyebrows and breathed deeply. Shifting her military jacket on her shoulders, she grasped the rail in front of her, the thin rose nails bending frailly before the onslaught of strength. The Duchess gazed out across the plain where slight flecks of snow still huddled in the shade of budding trees. In the distance a river lay as silver, cutting the blue mountains away from the plain. Her Highness threw out her arms in a luxurious stretch.

"God, but it's good to be alive!"

Lieutenant Mertz Komroff was shedding red silk and black leather upon his bunk where the garments sparkled under a shaft of sun which darted through the window into the wide room. Captain Kirvitch, as indolently as the smoke which rose from his long, perfumed cigarette, sat and regarded the slim youth stripping in front of him. He eyed the young body with pride.

"Damn it, Kirv," Mertz threw a crossbelt the length of the room. "I can't understand it! And I don't like it!"

"Now, now, my boy, don't let a little thing like that curl your hair. After all, what's one woman, more or less?"

"A woman in her position has no damned business making sheep eyes at one of her lieutenants. And I tell you, Kirv, she stood up there in full view of my men! In full view, I tell you! And looked at me!"

"Listen, Mertz, have you ever thought of why she gave you the commission you have framed up there?"

Komroff held a boot heel in one hand and stared frankly at the captain. "Why, why, because I had a good record at Moscow in school and because I have a fairly decent family tree in back of me."

The captain snorted disdainfully. "You think she picked you because of your family, eh? And because you had a good record? Why, man, I'll wager she never even knew you'd been to school in Moscow! Guess again!" He knocked his long cigarette against the bedpost. "I shouldn't really tell you because it might swell that head of yours. Most any woman could go crazy over you."

Mertz dropped a boot onto the floor and blushed. "I . . . I don't quite figure that out. What have I got?"

"If you were older I'd indict you for fishing for compliments." The captain ran his eye over the broad, flat back, flat stomach, the smooth flanks, the handsome profile. "What have you got!"

"You hadn't ought to talk that way, Kirv. After all, you know, I've a wonderful girl of my own." Komroff waved his hand toward the picture on his dresser.

The captain crushed his cigarette under a polished heel

and approached the bureau. "Yes, I've seen that before, my little one. And I've thought how damned lucky you were to have such a girl. How damned lucky you had a chance to make something of yourself for her sake. Does she really love you?"

Komroff straightened his shoulders. "Of course! Say, the last time I was home . . ."

"That's enough. I've heard all of that before two or three times. As I was saying, you're damned lucky to have a chance to make something of yourself."

"What do you mean?"

"Listen, boy, if you want anything in this Duchy, all you have to do is mind your cues, do a little forgetting, and try to make somebody else a little happy. Women especially; the women who really matter!"

"Wait a minute, Kirv. You know damned well I'd never cross my own girl."

"Wait a minute, be damned. If you want to be an ordinary lieutenant the rest of your life and always be so poor that you can't even send your own girl flowers on her birthday, go right ahead and be romantic. Go right ahead! You damned, pigheaded fool!"

Kirvitch toyed with a bunch of keys and continued. "Why, there are fully a hundred and fifty officers here who would give their right arms for the chance which is being handed to you all done up in blue ribbons with incense at midnight! And you stand there and tell me that you wouldn't cross your own girl!" The captain walked from the room and slammed the door behind him. Komroff listened to heels pound themselves down the hallway, into the distance, and then moved to his dresser.

"Never you mind, honey! It would take more than a world full of Kirvitchs and duchesses to make me hurt you!"

Her Highness inspected her face closely in her boudoir mirror, touching her hair tentatively.

"Not so bad, old girl," she informed the reflection, "not so bad. Of course you could look a little more innocent, but then, life is so trying, isn't it? Those sophisticated eyebrows now! How they persist in looking wise and worldly. Perhaps ever such a little touch of mascara might remedy that. And a little more on this side. Not so bad, old girl. He is handsome, isn't he?"

Her long fingers patted a velvet box which lay amidst a welter of makeup. "I've not seen so many who could refuse such, intelligently. Of course, he's a bit shy. His eyes this morning!" She laughed. "Olga!" she called to her maid. "The Ming pearls."

At the long window of her room, the Duchess paused and allowed her eyes to take in the panorama of the setting sun. She flung the door open and stepped out upon the balcony into the brisk evening wind. Bright and clean, cutting through her light gown, the wind brought her the fresh flavor of the tardy spring. She lifted her arms high over her head and her whole body tautened. The patrician arch of her firm, well-molded breasts was a veritable cupid's bow. Her slim fingers contracted like claws. "God, but it's good to be alive!"

Draped languidly upon a couch in the small dining room below, the Duchess ran approving eyes over the arrangement of the candles, Haviland china and gleaming silver. She placed an arm in back of her head and blew a column of blue smoke toward the tinted ceiling. In a far corridor, she could hear the even clamp of boot heels. "One, two, three, four! One, two, three, four!"

The insinuating voice of a sentry came to her through the opened door. "Your Highness! The Lieutenant Mertz Komroff!"

The cigarette in her hand described a brief arc and she heard a pair of heels click. Standing at stiff attention just inside the door, cap on forearm, red cloak swirling over his shoulder, a gleaming statue on which the candlelight played, stood the lieutenant. The sentry quietly closed the door.

"You may relax, Mertz. The sentry has gone." Her Highness waved vaguely at the foot of her couch. "Be seated!"

"Yes, Your Highness." Still holding his cap, Komroff sat delicately upon the edge of the sofa.

"Oh, by the name of Christopher and thirty other saints! Throw off that cloak; dash that cap to the floor! Relax!"

"Yes, Your Highness." Mertz did the bidding and then looked back at the reclining woman. He blushed becomingly.

"Cigarette, my dear? You may have heard that lighting one hides one's embarrassment. Are you rested after your rather strenuous campaign in the North?" She proffered a match, noticing the tip of his cigarette trembled slightly. "Ah, you brave men! You brave men! You slaughter a dozen armed devils with the haft of a broken sword without turning an eyelash. Confront you with a woman and you shake with ague! Come, my handsome one, tell me of your hopes and aspirations."

"They are few, Your Highness. Few and uninteresting. Especially to one in your high position."

"Call mine a high position?" She sat up and smiled at him. "What is position? What is this life, if it is without love?"

"Well," Mertz grinned suddenly. "Placed that way, it's pretty empty if you haven't ever come to love."

"Ah, I knew there was something more than sawdust in that fine head of yours. I have a confession to make to you tonight, Mertz. A deep confession. Do you mind?"

"Mind? But how could I? I am yours to command, otherwise, I should not be wearing these bars here." He touched his shoulder straps proudly and looked across the room to the fireplace.

"Bars! Bah! To hell with your shiny bars!" The Duchess reached out and snatched the straps, which tore away from his coat. "Now, my handsome one, you are no longer a lieutenant in my corps."

His cigarette dropped from his fingers to glow on the hardwood floor. "You mean, you mean . . ."

She laughed with suddenness. "No, not that. In many ways, my dear Mertz, you're an adorable fool." She pulled the bell rope and the door opened. "Boris! Bring the box on my boudoir table. Ah, yes, Mertz, you are an adorable fool at times." In silence, they awaited the return of the sentry.

Occasionally, Komroff's eyes dropped to his destroyed bars which lay upon the floor.

With the velvet box in her hands, the Duchess curled back cozily against the cushions.

"And now, before I tell you anything about this, I have a confession to make to you. I've lived here since I was a little girl. I've seen a thousand handsome officers come and go; I've met a dozen princes of great lineage and blood. But in all the years past, I have watched spring come, have seen it glow and burst into summer. I have rejoiced a little each year. Yes, a little. But it was not until a week ago that I understood the meaning of spring in full. A week ago, if you remember, you sat upon a nervous horse below my balcony, the young untried Lieutenant Komroff. And you swept your fine saber up to salute and smiled at me with your eyes. Since that time . . . At last I know what it is to walk out and meet the spring."

Mertz watched her with cautious eyes. "Yes, Your Highness."

"And now, my fine young blade, I have something for you far better than those." Her hand swept gracefully toward the torn straps on the floor. The velvet box sprang open to reveal two golden jeweled falcons. "The emblem, my dear, of a colonel in my corps." She reached out and placed the box in his hands.

He looked at it dully and then turned his gray blue eyes back upon her.

"Before I commission thee, my handsome one, I must exact the tiny payment of a kiss." She placed her hand in back of his head and seductively drew down his face to hers. The lieutenant, too dazed to resist, laid his lips full upon hers.

With a jerk he sat up straight and swept his hand back across his mouth. "My God! My God!" With an effort he recovered a little of his poise. "Your Highness, a word! I am in love with a girl in my own province. She thinks . . ."

"Bah!" Her voice was high-pitched. "You think more of a lowbred peasant woman than you do of a chance to make something of yourself? You think that by keeping those boyish lips untouched you can rise up to great heights in my service? You think that she can do more for you than I?"

Her voice, warm as the sun, was suddenly wheedling. "Come, my handsome one, forget such little things as that. Forget everything but the moment. Honor is not what it seems! I can give you so very much . . ."

Komroff stood up and laid the box on the table. Slowly he picked up his lieutenant's bars and placed them in his pocket. "With your permission, Your Highness, I shall leave."

Her Highness sat up very straight and looked coldly at her officer. "You may put those back where they were. You may remain in my service. But you shall live to regret the day you refused a kiss! Now go!"

In a sod hut on a far boundary of the Duchy of Novgrod, Lieutenant Mertz Komroff sat and stared listlessly at the wall. Captain Kirvitch swung an indolent pair of heels from the crude double bunk and watched blue smoke spiral from cigarette to ceiling.

"I'm going back tomorrow, Mertz, old boy. I guess Romski will be up to take my place." He dangled his heels awhile longer. "You know, Mertz, this makes your fourth month in this damned hole. Why in hell did you have to insult the old girl, anyway? Young, pretty, with a man's future in her hands. What in hell ever possessed you?"

Komroff's eyes stayed steadily upon the wall. "Let's not talk about that again, please!"

"All right, all right, but you know, for all your stubbornness, you may be here until doomsday. All you have to do is scribble a note down to her and say you know now that you acted a perfect ass. That's all and you could go back."

"To what?"

"God in heaven! Was there ever another like him?" Kirvitch shook his head sadly. "The longest a troop ever stayed here before was two weeks. After that, you run a chance of going nutty. And you've been here for four months! All because you wouldn't kiss a woman; a woman I'd make love to even if I saw her plowing in a field."

"We're a little different that way, I think. To you every cat is gray in the dark. After all, you know, this isn't so bad. The Cossacks from Njivi come nigh once in a while and cause a little excitement. What more can a man ask?"

"If you mean you find any fun in cutting down those lousy beggars, I know you're touched! Have a drink?" He poured out two brimming glasses of red wine and handed one to Komroff. "Come to think of it, one of the outposts mentioned a dust cloud about ten miles south of here. Might as well sound 'Boots and Saddles' just in case. Hell of a place to get cut down, this. No fair women in whose arms you can heroically and sadly die—or anything."

"Do you suppose Romski will bring any mail up?"

"Still worrying about that girl of yours, eh? Take a tip from me. She's undoubtedly run off with some peasant lad with a bag full of gold."

Komroff was suddenly very white. "Shut up!"

"All right, all right, you needn't get so wrought up. But if I hadn't heard from a girl for three months, I'd certainly think something was awry." Kirvitch walked through the door and looked back at Komroff. "You poor damned fool. All for the sake of a kiss!"

Captain Romski thundered in at midnight with a bag full of letters and a raging thirst.

"Thank God," said Kirvitch. "I'm glad to be out of this place."

"What's the matter?" asked Romski as he swung his long legs from the horse.

"Komroff! Another week with that fool, and I'd be crazy too."

"Still mooning about his girl, huh? Romantic, eh, Kirv? Exiled out here and wondering what in hell has happened to the light of his life." He glanced toward the door of the sod hut and saw Mertz. "Hello, you tramp," he called, moving toward the square of light on the bare ground, and throwing his reins to an orderly. "I think I have something important in the basket for you."

Mertz threw back his shoulders and grinned happily. "From . . ."

"Nope. Too many coats of arms on it for that!" Romski tossed the bag carelessly on the table and turned to pour himself out a drink. "That's a hell of a ride up here."

Komroff's trembling fingers poured the few letters out

on the bare table top and snatched up the two addressed to himself. With these in hand he lit the candle over his bunk and threw himself down. The seals on the large envelope stubbornly resisted him for a moment and then broke.

"My dear Lieutenant Komroff," it read. "It is my painful duty as the father of your betrothed to inform you that she has been dead these two nights past. . . . The physician was powerless against the onslaught of the poison. . . . Everything possible was done. . . . Cannot understand why . . . suicide always seems so far from those in the beauty of youth. . . . Left no word . . ."

The lieutenant stared as though hypnotized by the scrawl which covered the brown pages. Slowly the blood drained away from his face. He crumpled suddenly, crushing the letter beneath him. Romski and Kirvitch stared at him for a moment and remained wisely silent. The former drained his glass of wine and walked out of the bare hut, motioning for Kirvitch to follow.

"Whatever it is," said Romski, "it were better that he be left alone." He squatted on his heels against the wall and watched his cigarette glow in the dark.

"I was afraid of that." Kirvitch paced restlessly back and forth. "He's too damned young to have anything like that happen to him."

"You mean?"

"If you had watched Her Highness execute the agents from Kirsloff, you would not wonder long."

"Then the mail . . . ?"

"Has been held at the castle until now. The second envelope is ordering him back to the barracks for duty."

Romski shifted uneasily. "What kind of crude, rotten philosophy or logic would you call that?"

"Woman knows no logic, my dear captain. With the Duchy of Novgrod in the hideous state it is today, she plays with life and death for the dubious reward of a night of love."

A sentry ran up with his rifle at carry and forgot the formality of salute. "Captain! I just stumbled over outpost three. His throat's cut!" Cold terror vibrated from the trooper.

"The dust cloud!" Kirvitch unloosened his saber and set off at a run for the tents at the other side of the compound.

"Sacred ikons!" gasped Romski. "I wish my horse had gone lame!" He could hear Kirvitch shouting and threshing through the tents. The mutter of men startled from sleep swept as a wave across the camp.

Out in the night, a carbine cracked sharply and a bullet ricocheted above Romski's head. He hurled his cigarette from him and tore his revolver out of its holster. Silently he ran toward the tents.

The last outpost ran up out of breath and threw himself down at the end of the hastily formed line of men. Another carbine cracked and three rifles spurted flame in the direction of the flash.

Romski heard himself shout, "Hold that fire until they rush you!"

For the next few moments, the compound was terrifyingly still. Then hell broke loose.

A solid wall of deadly flame seemed to shoot in upon them from the north and the incessant rattle of the carbines filled all men's ears. The wall rolled closer as mounted men swept in upon the camp. All order was lost in a mêlée of hand-to-hand fighting. Horses impaled by uplifted sabers screamed. Now and then a point-blank shot lit up a distorted face.

The savage ring of steel on steel, punctuated by the cry of hit men, filled the darkness.

A hoarse, unsteady bugle bit out retreat, and the Cossacks were gone in a clatter of hoofs, leaving their dead and wounded behind them. Screams of the dying rent the air.

Kirvitch tripped over his own dead bugler and reaching down, wrenched the horn from its lanyard. The hysterical wail of "Boots and Saddles" brought the troopers rushing across the sod and the snorts of startled horses, saddled hurriedly in darkness.

Headlong, the troop of cavalry rushed out of the compound, eating the dust of the Cossacks. Up ahead, Romski leaned low over his horse's neck and strained his ears to catch the beat of iron on dirt far in front.

After a half-hour chase, the captain pulled up and brought his scattered troop to a stand. Save for the sob of deep-drawn breaths, the night was silent.

For a full minute, Romski listened and then, wheeling his horse, trotted back in the direction of the compound.

Lanterns glimmered here and there among the tents as wounded men dragged themselves about attending their fellows, sorting out the dead.

Kirvitch, wounded in the thigh, limped up beside Romski's horse. "Maybe the kid won't have to worry any more, after all."

"Dead?"

"No, but the crazy fool must have tried damned hard. A blade through the stomach."

While sentries reined their mounts back and forth on each side of the compound, Romski and Kirvitch entered the hut where Komroff lay upon the crude bed. His eyes were shut and his face was the color of slate. At the sound of footsteps, he opened his eyes and gazed disinterestedly at his two brother officers.

"Feel pretty bad?" Romski sat down on the edge of the bunk and threw his cap into a corner.

"Go away," muttered Komroff. "Can't you just go away and let me die?" His voice held the plaintive note of a child in pain.

"Why die? You'll be dead a hell of a long time." Kirvitch poured out a sparkling glass of wine and held it toward Mertz.

Komroff shook his head. "I don't care."

"You may not right now, but later on . . ."

Romski patted Mertz on the forehead. "Just concentrate a little and you'll be all right damned soon." He rolled up his sleeves. "And now let's redress and sew that wound."

Almost two months passed before Lieutenant Mertz Komroff was removed to the main barracks. There, seated among a welter of pillows in the window of his room, he stared out at the first snow of winter, his eyes expressionless, his face suddenly grown old.

A tree across the yard softly dropped leaf after leaf. Komroff watched them flutter to the ground.

Captain Kirvitch came into the room and brushed snow from his dark cloak. "How does it go, laddie?"

Komroff glanced at him and said nothing.

"Now is that any kind of welcome to give a fellow? I'll give you a drink and perhaps you'll feel a little better."

"No, thanks."

"Listen, old boy, if you wanted to you could get up out of that chair and run down two good horses. What's the use in just sitting there day after day and staring out that fool window? This is rather good stuff. Where did you get it?"

"Damn it; why ask? Her Highness sent up a hamper of it last night." The lieutenant's voice was dead and weary.

"Still interested in her young hero, is she? Why don't you give the old lass a break and make us step around here?" Kirvitch set the glass back on the table and noticed a note lying there. "What's this?"

Komroff looked at him blankly.

"How should I know?"

"Why, holy hell, you haven't opened it!"

"Read it if you like." Komroff turned his attention back to the falling snow and the tree.

"'My Lieutenant, Should you feel strong enough to do so, it would give me great pleasure to have your company, alone, tomorrow night at dinner.' Why don't you take her up on it?"

"What's the use?"

"My dear young fool. Have you no sense of gallantry?"

"I had too much, once."

40

"Pish, pish! Give the lady a chance, will you?"

"Did she send you up to say that?" Mertz threw back the blanket tucked around his knees. "All right, damn it! I'll go. I'll go!" He flung himself from the chair.

Kirvitch was for a moment taken aback by the vehemence of the statement. Recovering, "That's the way to talk! We'll have you for a commanding officer yet!"

Her Highness, the Duchess of Novgrod, thrust her shapely foot into a Paris slipper and smiled.

"The world does not stand for long against the onslaught of a clever woman, eh, Your Highness?" She buckled the strap and stood up, smoothing the flimsy dinner gown upon her long, beautifully curved flanks. "He comes without too much urging. It is well. Olga, where did you place that new perfume?"

She stood for a moment gazing out at the snow which filled the late afternoon. "Spring is so much more romantic, don't you think, Olga?"

Later she lay in the small dining room below, watching the flames lick up the chimney of the fireplace, and listening for the stamp of boot heels. Blue smoke drifted slowly from her nostrils. She was happy with anticipation.

From a far corridor came the unsteady tempo of a man walking slowly. The footsteps hesitated outside the door which swung open.

Dressed in plain blue and silver, Komroff stood in the threshold and looked steadily across the room at the Duchess. His eyes drifted to a velvet box which lay upon the table.

His eyes came back to Her Highness. "Good evening."

"Come in, handsome one." She smiled. "How's the poor old tummy getting along?" Her eyes lit up inquiringly.

"The tummy is all right." Komroff sat down in a chair at the head of the couch. "How is the colonel-making business these days?"

"Now, please don't be difficult, my dear. I look forward to a very pleasant little evening."

"The world has turned around many times since I last saw you, Your Highness."

"You poor boy. I knew you were just rusting to death up there in the barracks all by yourself. You'll like your new quarters."

"Perhaps, Your Highness. Though few men do."

A slight cloud came over the face of the Duchess and then cleared away. "Don't be silly. I'll have everything altered to please your slightest wish. Oh, but we're going to be happy!"

Komroff hitched his chair closer to the couch. "You know, dear lady, I have been thinking quite a little bit lately. I've had lots of time to think."

Something in his voice made the Duchess draw away a little. "You poor boy!"

"And it seems to me that a little coincidence of letters which occurred last spring points to a rather definite conclusion."

Her face whitened and she drew further away. The flame of passion died down.

Komroff placed his face very close to hers. "Do you know what I mean?" There was a fiery, sinister ring to his question.

"Why, how could I? You poor child. You have brooded too

much in your grief." She reached out with her left hand and laid it comfortingly upon his shoulder. Her right lay deep in the folds of the cushions.

He closed his hand slowly about her wrist and pulled it down to the side of the couch, smiling as he saw her wince. *"In some manner unknown to me, you killed my sweetheart!"*

"Lieutenant!" Her eyes blazed as those of a trapped, infuriated animal. She attempted to draw her hand out of his steel grasp.

Deliberately, he reached out and slapped her in the face. Throwing himself from her and out of the chair, he stood up. "I am going away now. I don't know where. Neither do I know how I can go and leave a thing such as you alive!"

Her right arm grew taut. The muzzle of a small automatic jutted out from the cushions. Komroff glanced at it and then smiled. "Well, Your Highness, why don't you?"

A spurt of flame bit deep into his face and he fell to the floor. Dully, he looked up at her above him. "God, but you're a rotten shot!"

Two sentries burst in through the doorway and gasped at the scene before them.

The Duchess threw the pistol down upon the couch. "Take this carrion out and throw it into a cell. Send Captain Romski here immediately."

The sentries dragged Komroff to his feet. Holding his bleeding face together, Komroff grinned through a red veil. "Have me shot and you'll save me the pain of getting this dressed."

A short time after the soldiers had left, Romski burst into the room. "What . . ." He clicked his heels and saluted. "At the orders of Your Highness."

"You will immediately organize a firing squad and *execute Lieutenant Komroff on the charge of assaulting me*!" She braced herself against the table and glared at Romski. "Immediately, I said!" She watched him turn on his heel. "And bury him without formality! Don't question my orders!"

Her breast heaved with emotion.

"Yes, Your Highness." He closed the door softly behind him and wandered down the corridor in a daze.

A half-hour later, the Duchess, crouched on the sofa, her eyes staring unseeing before her, heard the sharp commands of an officer and then the sudden blast of musketry in the back courtyard. She shuddered slightly and then shrugged. Standing at the window, she watched six troopers bear the wooden coffin out through the front gate toward the cemetery, their lanterns flickering dimly in the falling night.

But of all the barracks, only Romski and a sergeant knew that the wooden coffin which was hurried through the darkness, contained naught save a few hastily broken cobblestones and some earth.

Part Two: Aftermath

RUSSIA'S Revolution had almost become forgotten, save in the minds of those few White Russians who either sold their swords in the northern reaches of China or bartered their young bodies for gold, according to their sex.

Spring had drifted over the war-torn northern plains, and the land re-echoed with the marching feet of Chang Tso-Liang's trained men, when a small squadron of cavalry clattered down the streets of Nikwang, the men singing and the horses frisky in the brisk morning air.

At the head of the cavalcade, a White Russian slouched in his saddle and allowed his gaze to wander through the clusters on the sidewalks and into the richly filled stores. His blue gray eyes were dull, but a diagonal white scar, carved deeply by an almost forgotten bullet, gave his mouth a devil-may-care twist.

It was strange to see the town so well ordered and quiet after the recent anti-Communistic outbursts, for even yet, the beard-curling cry of "Communist!" was enough to send these people into swirling mobs of fiendish activity. Just a week before, in a seacoast town, Komroff had witnessed the spectacle of a young Chinese girl being stripped naked and torn bodily to bits on the supposition that she might be a Communist.

Secure in his title of Colonel in the Army of Chang Tso-Liang, Komroff wondered idly at the mischief he might do with that one voiced word. People on the sidewalk stared respectfully at the gray jackets and long lances, even though the sight was old to them. One warlord or another. It made so little difference to anyone.

Passing a gaudy hotel, Komroff chanced to let his gaze rest on the doorway. Several women of ill repute were there beckoning to him. His scar curved as he smiled at them. In his mind he jotted down the location of the building for later reference. The cluster of White Russian women appealed to men three days on the march.

But just as he was turning his head away, a familiarity of figure caught his eye. A startled face was gazing from within the doorway at him. Komroff straightened in the saddle and reined in his horse.

After staring for a moment and then shrugging his shoulders, he motioned for his Chinese sergeant.

"Take the men into camp on the other side of town. I shall join you later."

Hauling his muddy boot across the saddle, he dropped to the ground and made his way toward the hotel. Throwing the reins to a small Chinese boy, Komroff strode into the combination café and lobby.

Standing with her back against a far wall, a slim, attractive White Russian woman was staring at him with horror in her eyes.

Taking a chair near a window, Komroff beckoned to her and she came haltingly.

"Sit down, Your Highness!"

She stared at him and shuddered.

"I said 'Sit down!'" His blue gray eyes bored into hers.

"My God! How . . . how . . . ?" She collapsed weakly in a chair.

"Will you have a drink, Your Highness? Boy, two whiskey sodas! Chop-chop!"

"Komroff!"

"Is the world doing well by you these days, my dear Duchess? How is the colonel-making business?"

"But I thought . . ."

"That you had me executed. Well, Lazarus and I have resurrection in common. Your drink, Duchess, dear."

"Oh, God!" She buried her face in her arms. Komroff rose and quietly shook her shoulder.

"Come, where is your room? I said COME!" He jerked her to her feet and half dragged and then carried her across the café. The proprietor watched them climb the stairs and heard a door slam shut.

An hour later, Mertz Komroff stood at her door and contemptuously flung two silver dollars on the floor. "At that," he said, "you're a trifle overpaid."

Her former Highness crouched on the bed and stared at the money which sparkled against the dingy carpet. Suddenly her face straightened and she pressed a moist hand against her forehead. Opening the drawer of her dresser she lifted a heavy blue steel revolver from its place among her handkerchiefs and crept to the window.

Peering down in the street, she saw Komroff stride out of the café and place a foot in the stirrup of his saddle.

*He jerked her to her feet and half dragged and
then carried her across the café.*

Leveling the gun carefully, she took aim and pressed the trigger. The empty cartridge jumped back against the wall and a swirl of smoke curled around her head.

Below, Komroff slipped unsteadily into the saddle and looked up, conscious of a wet spot growing larger on his tunic. Suddenly he sat up straight and pointing his hand aloft, cried out a single word.

"Communist!" The cry reverberated and echoed up and down the crowded street. A madness seemed to engulf the crowd. People stopped, looked up, and seeing the face of the woman behind the smoking pistol, broke into a run.

Komroff smiled faintly as he watched them surge into the hotel, and then conscious of a growing weakness, slid from his horse to the street, where he stood for a moment. He gazed up at the window, made a slight gesture as though his hand held a saber, and crumpled, ceasing to hear the moan and roar of the crowd tearing madly into the tiny room of the hotel above him.

The Small Boss of Nunaloha

GET 4 FREE BOOKS!

You can have the titles in the Stories from the Golden Age
delivered to your door by signing up for the book club. Start today,
and we'll send you **4 FREE BOOKS** (worth $39.80) as your reward.

◄○►

The collection includes 80 volumes (book or audio) by master storyteller
L. Ron Hubbard in the genres of science fiction, fantasy, mystery, adventure and
western, originally penned for the pulp magazines of the 1930s and '40s.

◄○►

YES! ☑

Sign me up for the Stories from the Golden Age Book Club and
send me my first book for $9.95 with my **4 FREE BOOKS** (FREE shipping).
I will pay only $9.95 each month for the subsequent titles in the series.
Shipping is FREE and I can cancel any time I want to.

First Name	Middle Name	Last Name

Address

City	State	ZIP

Telephone	E-mail

Credit/Debit Card #: _____

Card ID# (last 3 or 4 digits): _____   Exp Date: _____/_____

Date (month/day/year) _____/_____/_____

Signature: _____

Comments: _____

Thank you!

The Small Boss of Nunaloha

"WONDER who that is?" Lanridge muttered audibly to himself. He had been watching the ship sail cautiously into the Nunaloha lagoon.

The light cream-colored sails fluttered idly against the deep blue sky as the strange schooner moved slowly into the lagoon and dropped anchor. The last thousand yards of water into the tiny natural harbor of the island of Nunaloha were filled with sandbars; only ships that had been there before could come through unguided. On her prow the word *Cora* stood out. Now the loud, imperative clang of the anchor chains rang out sharply.

Jim Lanridge, sitting lazily on his veranda, scowled at the ship. He hadn't been there long enough to know half the traders in the islands, but there was something insolent in the cut of this ship's jib, something that made him feel that its mission was not a peaceful one.

As representative of the Morely Trading Company on the isolated, lonely outpost that was Nunaloha, he had, of course, to meet the vessel with all courtesy. He rose, looking at the dark hull riding easily on the brilliant green swells of tropic sea. The water seemed to hush everything as it burst in soft cascades on the hot beach. He walked out to do the honors, after having momentarily debated and decided against taking down the gun that hung in a holster near him.

He was new to the job. An experienced South Seas hand could have known that from the way he walked, from the way he looked. Jim Lanridge wasn't what you'd call big; he stood a little over five feet six, and he was as lean and willowy as a rapier. Even in the glowing warmth of the tropical island he looked as if he might be cold. Lanridge had spent four years of his twenty-eight in Alaska. He had never forgotten that, and it had made him welcome this chance at Nunaloha with more enthusiasm than he had imagined he could have about anything. His light gray eyes might have shown that, too.

Hot sunlight and sweat, long drinks and easy chairs, babbling Melanesians trading with great cunning in the long post trade room—grinning wickedly with their filed teeth showing when they took away a bolt of yellow cloth in return for a small pearl—that had been his life for three months. He had begun to feel that someday he might really get the sunlight into his bones again, and he was happy. The solitude was nothing to him. He had known land so desolate that no life endured. Here there were the natives, the thousand things of air and land and sea. In the time he had been there, four ships had come to Nunaloha. . . .

And here was this vessel, which might be a trader.

A longboat was putting in to the shore. Men dressed in dirty whites were bending with the suppleness of the sea, leaving a trail of tiny whirlpools. In the stern, tiller in hand, stood a man naked to the waist. As the longboat grounded,

Lanridge saw the strength of the man, his great shoulders, his huge arms. His hair was a thick mat of black, and it half covered his torso. A brass buckle glinted against his brown skin, and the sun blazed in colored flashes of light from the handle of a revolver stuck carelessly in his waist.

The big man came swaggering forward, kicking up white foaming splashes of water, and then he walked ahead of the half dozen with him, his stride easy in the sand.

He came up to Lanridge and looked down at him, his eyes arrogant.

"Hello," said Lanridge. "If it's trade goods you've come for, I'm sorry; I'm full up. So if it's supplies you want, the only exchange we can use is money."

The big man frowned, then looked around at the other men who had come up to him, and suddenly he burst into a short laugh. They were an odd, ugly-looking lot—Chinese, dark men, light-skinned, all with the scars of battle. The big man's laugh died away as quickly as it had come. "I need food," he said, shortly. "I'm in a hurry."

"I'll have to see the money first."

The big man stood a moment, then said quietly, "How long are you here?"

"Three months."

The big man sighed. "Listen," he said, patiently. "I'm Big Pete Chambers. I'm the boss of the Banda Sea. I take what I want."

"And I'm the boss of Nunaloha," said Lanridge, his voice even as he looked up at the hulking Chambers. "Did you ever hear about the gunboats that come through here on piracy patrols?"

"There ain't been a gunboat big enough to get me yet," said Chambers. As if for silent corroboration, he glanced at the crew. A huge Chinese, his long mustachios hanging down past his chin, met Chambers' eye a moment, then went past him to Lanridge as Chambers added, "Now get your boys and do what I say!"

Lanridge was aware of an empty trading post behind him. He knew without looking that his brown aides had disappeared into the brush at the sight of the ship. In the momentary silence a yellow cockatoo sailed by and screamed.

"Beat it," said Lanridge. "Get back to your garbage scow." There was a peculiar quality in his voice, a monotonous tone.

For an instant, Chambers' hands trembled. Then he said, "Did you say something?"

"You heard me. Get out and stay out. I'm the boss on this island."

The big man's hands whipped up to the gun at his waist—and there they stopped. Plainly he was perplexed. You couldn't shoot down such a little fellow. It was obvious to everyone. A man shot an equal. The men from the boat were watching him; Chambers looked at them swiftly. Their faces were cold and brutal, but in their eyes a faint spark of interest glowed as they watched the scene.

Big Pete Chambers seemed to know it too. He took two steps forward. His huge fist lashed out and caught Lanridge on the side of his face. Lanridge went down into the sand without a sound. He fell as if he had been shot; he rolled over once and lay quietly.

He opened his eyes, crawled erect, and brushed the sandy hair from his eyes. Blood was coming from his cut lips. Then he spoke.

"Get off this island and get off quick."

Chambers had been about to start walking ahead. He had just started saying to his men, "Two of you go—" when Lanridge spoke. Now he whirled and stared at the little man. Lanridge was picking up his sun hat, and he was looking straight at Chambers.

Chambers turned a deep red under his sunned bronze. His lips curled back, and fairly leaping across the sand, he caught Lanridge by an arm, spun him about and smashed him across the face. Lanridge went down with a faint groan, his face buried in the sand.

"All right." Big Pete Chambers' voice broke the silence. "Fred," he said to a man almost his own size, a giant red-haired man with a short, broad nose, "you and Lonzo go into the warehouse. Pierre, take that gun down from the veranda. I'm going into this little nut's office and take—"

"You're not taking anything."

Jim Lanridge was standing on his feet again, a few yards away. His hands were at his sides, and the blood half covered his face. His eyes were narrow slits, and one of his cheekbones was raw and crimson.

The big man stood stock-still. "You dirty little b——," he said softly. And then he was walking deliberately toward

Lanridge, one hand fingering his gun. His face was contorted, half with disbelief at what was happening, half with rage. He came up close to Lanridge, looked at him.

"I got this job from a friend," said Lanridge. His voice was dead. There was no feeling in it. "I'm responsible for the stuff here, and neither you nor any other two-bit pirate is going—"

Chambers spat into Lanridge's face as he spoke. Jim Lanridge shot out a fist that hit Chambers on the bridge of his nose. He had just about time to raise his hand for another punch when Chambers' foot caught him in the abdomen. As he was falling Chambers crashed his forearm down across the little man's back.

This time Lanridge went down and stayed down. His mouth was partly open, and his breath came weakly as he lay unconscious on the beach. . . .

How long he had been out cold, Jim Lanridge didn't know. When he opened his eyes again, he was lying, trussed hand and foot, on a settee on the veranda. A few feet away, the men from Big Pete Chambers' schooner were passing back and forth, from the trading house to the longboat, and they were carrying whatever supplies Lanridge had had there.

Inside, in what Lanridge was pleased to call his office, he heard Chambers talking. ". . . breadfruit too. Get whatever there is in meat. I'll look through these papers and see what he's got booked in that warehouse."

Lanridge listened a moment, then wriggled, trying to free himself. Two of the sailors passed by him. They looked down at his face matted with dried blood, saw his half-closed swollen eyes looking up at them, and they watched Lanridge move around as if he were some queer, unhuman thing.

Lanridge's eyes were blazing as he looked up at the men. The taller of the two, the man called Fred, was staring incredulously at him. "Where did you get your guts, shrimp?" he said quietly. But he couldn't look into Lanridge's eyes.

"Lonzo," Fred said to his companion, "lend me that knife of yours a minute."

Lonzo's swart face smiled briefly. "No," he said, "I do it myself. I never see this before. I only think someday it happen. Maybe now."

And Lonzo bent swiftly over, knife in hand, and cut away the ropes that bound Lanridge. Without another word, they turned away and left. Lanridge watched them go. He sat a while, rubbing his chafed wrists.

Presently he walked into the trading room, and as he walked in Chambers looked up and saw him. The two men stood eyeing each other, and it was Chambers who spoke first. "Made up your . . ." and he stopped.

Pete Chambers seemed to be having difficulty speaking. He laughed, but there was a long pause between his laugh and the unfinished sentence, and the laugh had a hollow ring. Hurriedly then, looking away from Lanridge, Chambers growled, "Made up your mind to keep your trap shut?"

Lanridge sank into a chair. Chambers was running through a sheaf of papers he had taken from the desk. The somber Chinese came into the room just as Chambers began, "Hey, runt, what's this about—"

"You yellow-bellied rat," said Lanridge, softly. "Put those

papers down and get the hell off my island." He repeated, "Get the hell off."

Big Pete Chambers let his hand fall down, and the papers rustled. Lanridge could see him looking at the Chinese from the corner of his eye. The Chinese said nothing. He stooped for a sack of salt and went out.

"Do you want me to kill you?" Chambers said, but his voice was as quiet as Lanridge's had been, and his hands were nowhere near his gun. "You looking to get shot? Answer me, you lousy little runt!" His voice was rising now. "You want me to plug you? Talk up, you—"

"You won't shoot me. You know why you won't shoot me."

"What d'you mean?" Chambers cried, angrily. He came up close to where Lanridge was sitting.

"*Stay away from me!*" Lanridge called out, and he kicked out with a foot that just missed as Chambers jumped back. But his voice hadn't changed. "Keep away, you yellow rat," Lanridge said. "You know you're yellow."

"I'll kill you for that!" Chambers roared, his hand sliding up to his waist for the revolver. "Where the hell did you—"

"Put down those papers and clear out. Beat it."

Big Pete Chambers' face was livid. "I won't kill you. I'll whip you to a pulp. I'll break your back with my hands." He came up close to Lanridge and suddenly, before Lanridge could move his tired body again, he slapped him with the back of his hand. Once, twice, three times, and with each savage blow Lanridge's head swung about.

The big man backed away and looked at Lanridge, but

strangely, there was more pain on his face than on the little fellow's. "Shut up!" he shouted. "Shut up or I'll put a bullet through your head!"

Two men from the schooner entered, followed quickly by a third.

"What's up, Pete? We heard you yelling down the beach."

"Nothing."

"The little guy gettin' on your nerves, Pete?"

"Shut up!" Pete shouted, suddenly. "Get on with that loading. I'll take care of this."

Startled, yet not as much as they perhaps might have been, the sailors backed away and toted out more of the few remaining sacks.

"Hey, runt," said Chambers, after a time. "What's this note here on a letter about somebody bringing back pearls today?" He came up close to Lanridge again, then reached out gingerly and lifted the man's head. The eyes were open, looking at him. "Talk up or I'll give it to you again. Where you got these pearls?"

"Stick around a while," said Lanridge. "They're coming later this afternoon. You'll get yours. Old Aboo . . ." He couldn't finish.

Chambers brought Lanridge a glass of water. "Finish what you were saying," he said. "Finish, or I'll bust you in half."

"You'll never get those pearls. I'll tell you because I don't want you to be leaving just yet. Stick around. Old Aboo is bringing back the pearls he stole."

"Stole? Who'd he steal 'em from?"

61

"From the last trader here. He killed him and took the pearls. Now he's bringing them back. And there're a hundred of his best warriors coming with him."

"To hell with his warriors. What's he bringing them pearls back for?"

"Because I told him to. I said if he did I'd pay him in trade goods, and if he didn't I'd come up and get them anyway."

Chambers burst out, "Listen, runt, who you think you're talking to? What kind of stuff is this?"

"Nothing more than what I'm telling you. You'll never leave here with my goods, because I need them to pay Aboo. And you'll never get away with those pearls. You getting to know that too, aren't you?"

Chambers said nothing. He strode to the door of the large room, and standing on the veranda, he called out: "Manuel, get the boys together. Go back to the *Cora* and bring back those Tommy guns we been saving for a special occasion. I got the occasion invites just now." He laughed loudly.

But when he came in to Lanridge, he stopped laughing.

"You'll never get away," said Lanridge. "I'll get you. You've never met anyone who challenged you before. You're through."

Chambers' face was a pale mask as he listened to the slow, tenacious words in that dry voice.

It was toward twilight when the swarthy Manuel came running down the beach to where Chambers stood on the veranda of the trading house.

"Dey coming! Joe say he see maybe twenty canoe weeth islanders in them. 'Bout fifteen minute more to wait."

"All right," said Chambers. "Tell Pierre to take a couple of the boys and go into the brush over there. You take a few others and hold down that grove facing Pierre. I'll be here. When they start marching up the beach, come out one by one. If any of them make a move after we've warned them, give it to 'em. Be sure you've . . ." Chambers turned around and looked inside, scowling.

"Where'd the runt disappear to?" he said. From where Chambers stood he'd been able to see Lanridge sitting inside.

Manuel said, "What you say be sure we got?"

Chambers looked inside the trading house. Lanridge was on his feet, washing himself at a basin. He'd been eating, too; there were the remains of food on the table. Chambers stood there and looked on for moments; it was like watching a ghost coming back to life. Involuntarily, and furious with himself, Chambers shuddered.

"Hey, Pete," Manuel said, "what you worry 'bout that li'l shrimp so mahch?"

"Huh?" said Chambers, distantly, turning back. The words seemed to be sinking in moments later. "Worried? Me? Get on with what I told you." He stopped. "What the hell are you smiling about? Get!"

Ten minutes later, the long canoes appeared, riding high on a sea that had turned blue. In the purple twilight, their forms stood out against a faint ribbon of orange that lay across the horizon, and the splashes of their paddles were iridescent patches of greenish white.

The first of the canoes beached, and others followed. The natives, dressed in ceremonial costumes, many with their faces painted, raised their voices in excited conversation. Leisurely, an old man in their midst, with a huge flowered headdress, began walking toward the trading house. There were perhaps a hundred natives with him, jabbering away, jingling spears, swinging machetes playfully. It seemed as if the occasion were a holiday.

The natives had reached a point halfway between the shore and the trading house when Big Pete Chambers rose from the veranda and stood in plain sight on the steps. He had his revolver in hand, and he lifted it straight up. A warning shot smashed out, a harmless sound that was like a little thunderclap in its effect.

A great shout rose up from the natives. The old man in the middle gestured angrily, snatching a spear from a man near him. Then from the grove to the left, and the brush from the right, the sailors of Big Pete Chambers' crew appeared. The morbid-faced Chinese let his Tommy gun rattle a few times. The bullets plowed a furrow in the sand a few feet in front of the old island chieftain.

"Aie-eee!" It was a battle cry. Half a dozen spears flew at the Chinese, standing just a bit before the others from the grove.

The machine gun spat out a horizontal line of gold-flecked flame. Two of the natives jerked off their feet and fell suddenly. A third screamed, clutching his abdomen. He spun around once and fell thrashing to the sandy beach, screaming in wild agony until his voice died in a gurgle.

The beach had become discolored with dark stains.

Suddenly Big Pete Chambers plunged forward and pitched off the stairs, his face hitting into the sand. Close behind him, the little body of Jim Lanridge followed. Lanridge had come out of the trading room, taken one swift glance at Chambers and smashed into him, with his body thrown like a bullet, crashing into Chambers' back, throwing him.

Quickly, Lanridge rolled over and gripped Chambers' arm, fastened it behind the big man's back. With a surge, Chambers broke the hold and rolled out, dragging Lanridge with him.

Jim Lanridge was a beautiful target for any one of half a dozen Tommy guns, sitting half astride Pete Chambers' back for an instant, but no gun fired. The crew of the *Cora* stood watching the short struggle in the sand without lifting a hand. There were glances exchanged by many of them. The giant Fred watched intently.

A native leaped out from the group and advanced toward the two figures which were rolling in the sand. Two guns and a rifle sang together. The native stopped, looking foolish in death, and slumped abruptly into the sand. It had become clear that the intent of the crew of the *Cora* was to let the fight go on unhindered. Once, Manuel said, "De runt, he is *el diablo.* I wonder what happen next weeth heem around. I wonder all day."

Chambers' fists were flailing Lanridge. He was holding the smaller man by a handful of shirt and bringing a fist like a hammer down on Lanridge's skull. And out of the silence that had come when the two men grappled, a silence broken for a second by the short burst of fire, came Chambers' voice, a horrible roaring, throaty sound, full of fury and desperation.

It didn't last long. Jim Lanridge shot his arms like pistons, whipping short, ineffectual blows to Chambers' abdomen, and then he went down. Chambers stood over him and kicked. Lanridge seized the leg that crushed into his ribs and pulled. Chambers tumbled forward and fell on Lanridge. Lanridge wrapped a thin arm around Chambers' throat. One of Chambers' hands ripped the arm away and he rolled to one side. He started to rise, and Lanridge, rising more quickly, hurled himself forward again and rammed into Chambers' side.

Strangely, a sob tore out of Chambers as he rolled away again. His huge arm reached out and his hand gripped Lanridge's sandy hair. He pulled Lanridge for inches by his hair and then he was punching him wherever he could strike a blow.

Chambers' face was like a demon's. His eyes were bloodshot and watery, and the spittle had run out his lips. Words kept pouring from him, meaningless, choking words, softly, almost crying. "I'll kill you," he kept saying, over and over. "Say you've had enough—*say enough!*"

Then suddenly, as Lanridge was quiet, with only his eyes staring at Chambers, the big man looked around him. He was isolated. He was alone in his struggle with this little man.

Lanridge whispered, "You'll never get away."

Chambers rose slowly to his feet, walked back to the veranda and picked up the revolver that had been flung from his grasp. The weariness lay on him like a weight. His gait was tired, his face haggard. He held the revolver and walked by Lanridge without looking at him.

He came up close to the old man among the natives, and his crew walked in with him. The natives edged back. The old chief stood out alone, and in his hands he carried a small leathern bag.

Big Pete put his gun into the old man's belly and took the bag away from the bony hands that yielded it. He stepped away and opened the bag in his palms. A small fortune in pearls rolled into his hands, tiny, cloudy-white spheres that seemed to glow.

But there was no pleasure in Chambers' eyes. He looked at the pearls dully, hardly seeing them, and put them back into the bag with trembling hands. Then his eyes went sideways to look at Lanridge, lying on the sand. But Lanridge wasn't there!

Chambers whirled, gasping, almost crying out again. Jim Lanridge was standing a few feet away. He was just standing there, a thin little fellow in the gathering darkness, his face torn and bloody, his clothes half in rags, but there was something unreal about him, something beyond comprehension. It stood out in the way Chambers had spun about, to see just this small man standing there. The sweat ran down Chambers' face in long rivulets. He turned away violently.

"Those pearls are company property," came the dead voice. Chambers started, and the bag of pearls in his hand almost fell to the sand. "I live on this island. These natives trust me. Get your men to bring back the stuff they took, and turn those pearls over to old Aboo."

For a moment Chambers said nothing. Then he turned to Pierre and muttered, "Let's go. We've got what we came for."

"What about the runt?" the man Fred drawled. "Gonna let—"

"What about him?" Chambers shouted. His voice was unnaturally loud. "We've got what we wanted. To hell with him!"

"You leave him standing up after what he say?" Manuel said, quietly. Perhaps there was a faint trace of sarcasm in his words.

"I'm boss here!" Chambers roared. "What I say goes."

"Yeah," Fred said. No one could be sure whether it was a question or not.

Guns at their sides, the crew of the *Cora* moved down the beach to their longboat. Lanridge came closer to the natives and watched the longboat pull away.

Aboo, the chieftain, began to babble something. "You know I don't understand you," said Lanridge, patiently. "Wait here. They can't get away. It's too dark to try getting past the sandbars in the lagoon."

Now the natives began to jabber all together, running about the chief and gesturing, pointing to Lanridge. The chief raised his thin voice, and the noise was subdued. Old Aboo took Jim Lanridge's battered face in his withered hands, turning it this way and that, and he kept talking. No man took such a beating if he was an accomplice to a robbery. It was too real to disbelieve.

Lanridge stood patiently a moment, then turned away. Several of the natives had started a fire on the sandy shore. He stood in the darkness and heard the distinct clang of anchor chains being drawn up. Peering, he saw the pale sails of the *Cora* fluttering aloft. Big Pete Chambers was going to try getting out of Nunaloha in the dark.

Then Lanridge was trotting to where the Melanesians had beached their canoes. He got into one, pushed off and began to paddle quietly.

The *Cora* was beginning to move when Lanridge came alongside. He swung his canoe until he had fallen behind to the after side, then he paddled along for some moments, staying close to the rudder, making no sound.

He kept his eyes glued to the fire on the beach, keeping his bearings by watching where the light went to. Presently he drew closer to the rudder, and then suddenly he swung the canoe sharply into the side of the ship, smashing the strong prow of his canoe into the huge blade of the rudder.

The rudder wavered for an instant, and in that instant Lanridge had come leaping forward to jump out and seize the rudder, swinging on the heavy geared chain, dragging it down for a surprising moment with his weight. The rudder veered sharply right.

Overhead, on the deck of the *Cora*, a series of oaths rang out. The chain swung back as the man at the wheel turned, and the rudder whipped back to position.

Then, all at once, a shudder went through the schooner. The whole ship trembled softly and stopped moving. That instant of veering had caught her prow firmly in one of the sandbars that had formed a channel through which the ship was passing.

Lanridge had dropped off the chains as the rudder had swung back. Slowly he swam to the canoe nearby, and holding on to the sides, came alongside the vessel. He found one of the rope ladders leading down, and climbed up.

Big Pete Chambers was roaring on the bridge. The Chinese stood by impassively, a lamp lighting his features. Manuel was shouting down at a group of men who stood close to the rail, looking over the side. The confusion was gathering when Lanridge walked into the light.

"I've come for the pearls," he said, starting to walk up on the bridge. The man nearest him, Pierre, gasped and stood back. Every eye had leaped to Chambers. "You'll never get away," said Lanridge. "You're on a sandbar and it'll take a strong wind to get you off."

Big Pete Chambers stood as if paralyzed, making no move until Lanridge was close to him. Then his hand went to the gun stuck in his waist, and it came out, ugly, blue-barreled, glinting in the half-light. Chambers' lips were thin and dry as he brought the gun up. In the tense silence, the click of the trigger cocking back smacked out.

The man named Fred, standing beside Chambers, put out a hand. His face was blank as he spoke. "Put the gun away, Pete. The boys don't like to have any more murders pinned on them than is necessary. Sometimes the boss of this ship don't need a gun—or maybe he ain't the boss."

Chambers' hand held back, while his gaze swept the men standing around, silent spectators. "I said I'd kill him," Pete said. "Don't you see? I got to kill this . . ." Without warning, with a hoarse cry, Chambers had twisted the gun around in his hands and lunged at Lanridge. He swung the butt end and caught Lanridge on the temple. . . .

Chambers let the gun drop from his hand. He couldn't face

the men who ringed him. He rubbed a hand across his face, pressing his fingers into it. "He ain't human," he whispered, and the whisper carried sibilantly in the wind.

Still no one said anything. Lanridge lay quietly at Manuel's feet.

"I said I'd kill him!" Chambers shouted. "You hear me? I told him I'd kill him. It's either him . . ."

In the continuing silence, where men only looked, Chambers swung down to Lanridge's inert body, lifted him up. He ran down from the bridge, carrying the little man to the side.

He raised his arms high and flung the still body overboard.

Then he sat down by the rail.

Jim Lanridge came to with his lungs half full of water. He coughed, retching. There was ground under his feet; he was lying half submerged on a sandbar. Looking up, he saw the huge dark form of the *Cora*. He kept coughing up water for half an hour. His head felt heavy, his temples were pounding. A probing hand found an unclotted wound there.

He could hardly move, yet he forced himself off the sandbar, floating in the water, with an occasional kick, propelling himself to the schooner. He found the ladder over the side again.

There was no one in sight when he stood on the deck. The bridge was deserted. He walked to the fo'c's'le, and heard men's voices. Then he climbed down the stairs.

In the lighted crew room sat Chambers and his men, and

on the table before them lay the pearls that old Aboo had brought. When Lanridge started down the stairs, they heard him. Chambers rose from his seat and the chair fell away. His eyes were wide in terror. A hand was flung up before his face. Lanridge stood there, a little battered man, his clothes wringing wet, his light hair pressed against the blood on his face. Silently he began walking toward Chambers, like a wraith from the sea.

A great cry, like the sound of a wounded man, a man in agony, tore from Chambers' lips. His eyes were closed. Someone near him pushed him forward. "God," he screamed, stopping. "Get him away! Get him away!"

He tore a revolver from a coat pocket. Three hands grasped his own. Manuel, Pierre, Fred, stood there.

"Not the gun," said Lonzo, distinctly. "We don't like it."

Fred's eyes were shining like jewels. "The boss of the Banda Sea?" he said.

Pierre reached out and took the gun from Chambers.

All three stepped back, leaving the two men alone again.

Chambers lunged forward blindly. A stinging hand came up into his face before his body crashed against Lanridge again, pressing him to the wall until Lanridge's head cracked sharply against the beam behind him.

When he backed away, Lanridge fell to the floor like an empty coat might have fallen. . . .

Chambers stood there, looking down, and then brokenly he dragged himself to one of the bunks and fell heavily on it. His fists were weakly pounding down on the bed; his heavy frame was wracked by great sobs.

"Get up," Pierre ordered him.

Chambers heard Pierre's deadly monotone. Slowly he raised his head, his swollen eyes slits of horror.

Jim Lanridge was getting up also. His body was pressed against the wall, but he was rising. And his face was terrible, his light eyes staring, burning, his lips clenched.

Then he was walking toward Chambers. The huge man screamed horribly and rolled off the bed, half falling to the floor. He stood there, one knee on the floor, while the men stood around in grotesque muteness, backing away as Lanridge came forward.

Lanridge came up to him. He lifted a foot, held it against Chambers' side and pushed him over. The floor shuddered, and the only sound was Chambers' breathing in huge tortured gasps. He lay on his back, his face contorted, his lips covered with drying foam, looking up dumbly at Lanridge.

Silently, Lanridge reached out, gathered up the little leathern sack of pearls from the table. Then he knelt beside Chambers and ran his hands through the fallen man's coat. He took out a dirty leather wallet and began counting out green bills. The rest he put back in the wallet, and threw the wallet to the floor.

Lanridge turned and started up the stairs. Halfway up he heard Chambers scream something incoherently, and then it was quiet.

When he was out on the deck he heard someone behind him.

It was Fred. They stood together a moment and Fred said, "I'll take you ashore in a boat."

His body was pressed against the wall, but he was rising.
And his face was terrible, his light eyes staring,
burning, his lips clenched.

"No," said Lanridge. "I've got my own boat. I'm the boss of Nunaloha. Stay away from my island."

He brushed a hand across his battered face, swayed uncertainly a minute. Then he recovered and climbed over the side, going down to the canoe below.

Minutes later, the crew of the *Cora*, standing along the rail in utter silence, could hear him paddling away in the darkness. . . .

Story Preview

NOW that you've just ventured through some of the captivating tales in the Stories from the Golden Age collection by L. Ron Hubbard, turn the page and enjoy a preview of *Destiny's Drum*. Join adventurer Phil Sheridan as he boldly and shrewdly enlists the help of native headhunters to drive out a predatory local regime and put an end to a reign of tyranny in the southern seas of Indonesia.

Destiny's Drum

JOSÉ EMANUEL BATISTA'S voice flowed on like a river of crude oil—conversational, ingratiating in spite of the portent of his words.

"And then, *senhor*," said *Governador* Batista, "what may I be expected to do? You come here, attack my poor soldiers, laugh at them, and then refuse to state the reason you come to Kamling. What am I to believe?"

The white man, who lounged in the battered wicker chair on the other side of the more battered pine desk, returned no answer. His eyes were fastened on something outside the thatched hut.

The *governador* leaned forward. "And if, *senhor*, you are an international spy, come to survey the fortifications, I find it necessary to shoot you without delay. And if you are the only other thing you can be, an outlaw, also must I shoot you. In fact, *senhor*, I think it is best that I order out my firing squad immediately."

The white man sat up a little in his chair, still staring out the door. "What," he said, "is the name of that white girl out there?"

The *governador*'s smoothness fell away from him. An exasperated light entered his black, beady eyes. His several chins lopped over the edge of his white jacket collar and quivered there. It appeared that he had been struck a mortal blow.

The girl in question had swung down from her horse and had entered the trading post. Dust swirled in small geysers where her riding boots had left their imprint.

The white man turned, then, to give the *governador* more particular attention. "Now what was that you were talking about?"

The *governador*'s bushy brows were drawn down tight and his spiked mustache stood straight out from the round swarthy ball which was his face.

"*Senhor,*" he said, "you are insulting to my dignity of office."

"What office?"

"What office? *¡Por Dios!* Have you no respect whatever? The office of *governador* of the island of Kamling, jewel of the Banda Sea."

"Oh." A pack of black cigarettes lay on the *governador*'s desk. Taking one, the white man looked innocently into the official's face. "Have you a match?"

José Emanuel Batista sighed as quietly as possible and passed a paper package to the white man, a rugged young man in tattered white sailor pants. The young man's eyes were infinitely blue, infinitely languid. He was plainly bored.

"Let me go over this again, *senhor.* It is plain that you do not understand what you face. A firing squad!" The *governador* waved a dramatic hand across the street to a white wall.

"Is that all? *Governador,* it is much too warm to argue. If I am an international spy, shoot me. And if I am an outlaw, shoot me. But, for heaven's sake, don't talk so much!" He dragged upon the cigarette and braced his feet against the door jamb. The flimsy hut rocked perilously.

Once more the *governador* sighed. He glanced up at the face of the native who stood beside him. That face was brown, mostly filed teeth and lusterless eyes. The chin was resting on a naked wrist and the hand was holding a long, sharp spear. This was Aboo-Tabak, King of Kamling, though his regal robes consisted of a breechcloth and his badge of office was nothing more than a luminous-dialed, loudly ticking alarm clock which dangled about his scrawny throat.

"Aboo-Tabak," said the *governador*, "this man has insulted your office, my office, and the authority invested in us. What shall we do with him?"

"Eat him."

The white man laughed and took another drag from the black cigarette. "The government of Portugal forgot about this island thirty years ago and they've probably forgotten all about you as well."

"Continue!" ordered the *governador*.

"All right. I'll add that you're former Sergeant Duarte of the island of Timor, wanted for murder and a few other things. And that you blackbirded along here for a while known as Portuguese Joe."

"How do you know these things?"

The white man yawned and readjusted his feet. He kept a weather eye on the door of the trading post.

"I know them, that's all," he said. "Otherwise you wouldn't care whether I landed here or not, and you wouldn't put yourself to such great pains to shoot me. Although you haven't asked it yet, my name is Sheridan."

The *governador*'s eyes glittered with amazement. "Sheridan!" he croaked. "Sheridan of the Nineteenth Route Army? That Sheridan?"

"I blush to admit it."

José Emanuel Batista sat back, rubbing his moist, fat palms together. "Then there is a chance that some of your rich friends might wish to buy you back again!"

"Not a chance. Go ahead and shoot me if you want. I'm tired of this."

"But wait," said the *governador*. "There is something you might do which would purchase your liberty."

"What?"

"Up above the town, three or four miles back from the edge of the sea, *senhor,* there is a man that causes me trouble."

"And," supplied Sheridan, "you want me to kill him for you."

"That's right."

"And what's he got that you want?"

"Oh, nothing, nothing, *senhor*. Has he, Aboo-Tabak?"

The King of Kamling shifted his weight on the spear. "Girl, gold. Sure, you want lots along that feller."

José Emanuel Batista smiled a sick smile. "He's lying, Sheridan. He gets those ideas now and then. The sun, you see."

Sheridan snorted. "Having heard a few stories about this Portuguese Joe, I'd rather believe a cannibal."

"Cannibal!" barked Aboo-Tabak, leaning forward on the spear. "I be Muslim, praise Allah!"

Sheridan grinned, though the dead viciousness in

Aboo-Tabak's eyes hardly invited such an expression. "But," said Sheridan, "if you're a follower of Allah, then why do you let yourself be ruled by an infidel dog of a Christian?"

"That's enough of that!" roared the *governador*, jumping to his feet.

Aboo-Tabak's eyes lingered on Portuguese Joe's fat shoulders which threatened to burst through the white duck jacket.

"Well, why?" insisted Sheridan.

Aboo-Tabak smiled, displaying yellow, pointed teeth. "He say someday he take me to town called . . . called . . ."

"Paris," supplied José Emanuel Batista, sitting down again. "Now, *senhor*, to return to our business again. As long as you refuse to kill this man for me, I see no other course but to let my regiment execute you. After all, *senhor*, you came here this morning, landed and immediately quarreled with my men."

"They tried to take my money and guns from me."

"That is a severe charge against my troops, *senhor*. You infer that they are bandits, eh?"

"Certainly," agreed Sheridan cheerfully. "But hold this up a moment, will you? The girl is coming out of the trading post."

The *governador* jumped up, almost upsetting his desk. He started out the door, but Sheridan's raised feet blocked him. With a grin Sheridan lowered the offending legs and stood upon them. He was almost a foot and a half taller than Portuguese Joe.

Across the street two soldiers rose up from their place at the base of the wall. They cradled their rifles across their arms and watched Sheridan with sleepy eyes.

The girl had mounted the small pony, after tying a bag of supplies behind the saddle. She cantered toward the group which stood in the sun waiting for her. At first it appeared that she would pass by without a glance. Then she caught sight of Sheridan and pulled up.

To find out more about *Destiny's Drum* and how you can obtain your copy, go to www.goldenagestories.com.

Glossary

STORIES FROM THE GOLDEN AGE *reflect the words and expressions used in the 1930s and 1940s, adding unique flavor and authenticity to the tales. While a character's speech may often reflect regional origins, it also can convey attitudes common in the day. So that readers can better grasp such cultural and historical terms, uncommon words or expressions of the era, the following glossary has been provided.*

Banda Sea: the sea of the south Moluccas (a group of about one hundred and fifty islands) in Indonesia, technically part of the Pacific Ocean but separated from it by the islands.

blackbirded: engaged in the slave trade, especially in the Pacific.

"Boots and Saddles": a bugle call alerting cavalrymen to put on their riding boots and saddle their horses. There are many different bugle calls, each with its own meaning and essential to all military communication. The enlisted soldier's life was regulated by them. The primary bugler was assigned to the headquarters staff and kept close to the commander at the front.

carbine: a short light rifle; originally used by soldiers on horseback.

Cossack: a member of a people of Southern European Russia and adjacent parts of Asia, noted as cavalrymen, especially during tzarist times.

curb bits: bits used to control a horse's action by means of pressure on the reins. A curb bit consists of the actual bit with a chain or strap attached, passed under the horse's jaw.

devil-may-care: wildly reckless.

el diablo: (Spanish) the devil.

fo'c's'le: in merchant vessels, the forward part of the vessel, under the deck, where the sailors live.

G-men: government men; agents of the Federal Bureau of Investigation.

governador: (Portuguese) governor.

Haviland: Haviland & Co, established in 1842 in Limoges, France. The company is known for its fine china with hand-painted and custom designs.

Hudson Bay: a large inland sea in the northeast of Canada. On the east it is connected with the Atlantic Ocean and on the north with the Arctic Ocean.

hummock: a ridge or hill of ice in an ice field.

igdlu or *igdlut:* (Eskimo) igloo or igloos; an Eskimo house, usually made of sod, wood or stone when permanent, or of snow and skin when temporary.

jib: small foremost sail; a small triangular sail in front of the main or only mast on a sailing ship or sailboat.

kamik: (Eskimo) a knee-high waterproof boot with a hard sole, made of sealskin.

Lazarus: a man whom Jesus raised from the dead.

Lee-Enfield: a standard bolt-action magazine-fed repeating rifle; the British Army's standard rifle for over sixty years from 1895 until 1956, although it remained in British service well into the early 1960s and is still found in service in the armed forces of some Commonwealth nations.

longboat: a large boat that may be launched from a sailing ship.

Melanesians: people native to a division of Oceania in the southwest Pacific Ocean, comprising the islands northeast of Australia and south of the equator. It includes the Solomon Islands. The Melanesian people primarily fish and farm, and supplement their economy by exporting cacao, copra (coconut) and copper.

por Dios: (Spanish) for God's sake.

rapier: a small sword, especially of the eighteenth century, having a narrow blade and used for thrusting.

rudder: a broad, flat, movable piece of wood or metal hinged vertically at the stern of a boat or ship, used for steering.

Russia's Revolution: the rebellion in Russia in 1917 that occurred in two stages, the first leading to the overthrow of the tzarist government and establishment of a provisional government (March 1917) and the second, replacing this government with the Soviet government led by Lenin (November 1917) that led to a period of civil war that ended in 1922.

saber chain: a chain on an officer's uniform, worn on the left side at waist level, to which the scabbard is attached.

Scheherazade: the female narrator of *The Arabian Nights,* who during one thousand and one adventurous nights saved her life by entertaining her husband, the king, with stories.

schooner: a fast sailing ship with at least two masts and with sails set lengthwise.

scow: an old or clumsy boat; hulk; tub.

senhor: (Portuguese) a title of courtesy equivalent to *Mr.* or *sir.*

Timor: an island at the south end of a cluster of islands located between mainland southeastern Asia and Australia. The island has been politically divided in two parts for centuries: West Timor, which was known as Dutch Timor from the 1800s until 1949 when it became Indonesian Timor; and East Timor, which was known as Portuguese Timor from 1596 until 1975.

Tommy guns: light portable automatic machine guns.

White Russians: Russians who fought against the Bolsheviks (Russian Communist Party) in the Russian Revolution and fought against the Red Army during the Russian Civil War from 1918 to 1921.

Yukon Territory: the westernmost of Canada's three territories, it is positioned in the northwest corner, bordering Alaska. Yukon is known as "the land of the midnight sun" because for three months in summer, sunlight is almost continuous. In winter, however, darkness sets in and the light of day is not seen for a quarter of the year.

L. Ron Hubbard
in the Golden Age
of Pulp Fiction

*In writing an adventure story
a writer has to know that he is adventuring
for a lot of people who cannot.
The writer has to take them here and there
about the globe and show them
excitement and love and realism.
As long as that writer is living the part of an
adventurer when he is hammering
the keys, he is succeeding with his story.*

*Adventuring is a state of mind.
If you adventure through life, you have a
good chance to be a success on paper.*

*Adventure doesn't mean globe-trotting,
exactly, and it doesn't mean great deeds.
Adventuring is like art.
You have to live it to make it real.*

— *L. RON HUBBARD*

L. Ron Hubbard
and American
Pulp Fiction

B ORN March 13, 1911, L. Ron Hubbard lived a life at least as expansive as the stories with which he enthralled a hundred million readers through a fifty-year career.

Originally hailing from Tilden, Nebraska, he spent his formative years in a classically rugged Montana, replete with the cowpunchers, lawmen and desperadoes who would later people his Wild West adventures. And lest anyone imagine those adventures were drawn from vicarious experience, he was not only breaking broncs at a tender age, he was also among the few whites ever admitted into Blackfoot society as a bona fide blood brother. While if only to round out an otherwise rough and tumble youth, his mother was that rarity of her time—a thoroughly educated woman—who introduced her son to the classics of Occidental literature even before his seventh birthday.

But as any dedicated L. Ron Hubbard reader will attest, his world extended far beyond Montana. In point of fact, and as the son of a United States naval officer, by the age of eighteen he had traveled over a quarter of a million miles. Included therein were three Pacific crossings to a then still mysterious Asia, where he ran with the likes of Her British Majesty's agent-in-place

L. Ron Hubbard, left, at Congressional Airport, Washington, DC, 1931, with members of George Washington University flying club.

for North China, and the last in the line of Royal Magicians from the court of Kublai Khan. For the record, L. Ron Hubbard was also among the first Westerners to gain admittance to forbidden Tibetan monasteries below Manchuria, and his photographs of China's Great Wall long graced American geography texts.

Upon his return to the United States and a hasty completion of his interrupted high school education, the young Ron Hubbard entered George Washington University. There, as fans of his aerial adventures may have heard, he earned his wings as a pioneering barnstormer at the dawn of American aviation. He also earned a place in free-flight record books for the longest sustained flight above Chicago. Moreover, as a roving reporter for *Sportsman Pilot* (featuring his first professionally penned articles), he further helped inspire a generation of pilots who would take America to world airpower.

Immediately beyond his sophomore year, Ron embarked on the first of his famed ethnological expeditions, initially to then untrammeled Caribbean shores (descriptions of which would later fill a whole series of West Indies mystery-thrillers). That the Puerto Rican interior would also figure into the future of Ron Hubbard stories was likewise no accident. For in addition to cultural studies of the island, a 1932–33

LRH expedition is rightly remembered as conducting the first complete mineralogical survey of a Puerto Rico under United States jurisdiction.

There was many another adventure along this vein: As a lifetime member of the famed Explorers Club, L. Ron Hubbard charted North Pacific waters with the first shipboard radio direction finder, and so pioneered a long-range navigation system universally employed until the late twentieth century. While not to put too fine an edge on it, he also held a rare Master Mariner's license to pilot any vessel, of any tonnage in any ocean.

Yet lest we stray too far afield, there is an LRH note at this juncture in his saga, and it reads in part:

"I started out writing for the pulps, writing the best I knew, writing for every mag on the stands, slanting as well as I could."

To which one might add: His earliest submissions date from the summer of 1934, and included tales drawn from true-to-life Asian adventures, with characters roughly modeled on British/American intelligence operatives he had known in Shanghai. His early Westerns were similarly peppered with details drawn from personal

Capt. L. Ron Hubbard in Ketchikan, Alaska, 1940, on his Alaskan Radio Experimental Expedition, the first of three voyages conducted under the Explorers Club flag.

experience. Although therein lay a first hard lesson from the often cruel world of the pulps. His first Westerns were soundly rejected as lacking the authenticity of a Max Brand yarn (a particularly frustrating comment given L. Ron Hubbard's Westerns came straight from his Montana homeland, while Max Brand was a mediocre New York poet named Frederick Schiller Faust, who turned out implausible six-shooter tales from the terrace of an Italian villa).

Nevertheless, and needless to say, L. Ron Hubbard persevered and soon earned a reputation as among the most publishable names in pulp fiction, with a ninety percent placement rate of first-draft manuscripts. He was also among the most prolific, averaging between seventy and a hundred thousand words a month. Hence the rumors that L. Ron Hubbard had redesigned a typewriter for faster keyboard action and pounded out manuscripts on a continuous roll of butcher paper to save the precious seconds it took to insert a single sheet of paper into manual typewriters of the day.

That all L. Ron Hubbard stories did not run beneath said byline is yet another aspect of pulp fiction lore. That is, as publishers periodically rejected manuscripts from top-drawer authors if only to avoid paying top dollar, L. Ron Hubbard and company just as frequently replied with submissions under various pseudonyms. In Ron's case, the

A MAN OF MANY NAMES

Between 1934 and 1950, L. Ron Hubbard authored more than fifteen million words of fiction in more than two hundred classic publications. To supply his fans and editors with stories across an array of genres and pulp titles, he adopted fifteen pseudonyms in addition to his already renowned L. Ron Hubbard byline.

Winchester Remington Colt
Lt. Jonathan Daly
Capt. Charles Gordon
Capt. L. Ron Hubbard
Bernard Hubbel
Michael Keith
Rene Lafayette
Legionnaire 148
Legionnaire 14830
Ken Martin
Scott Morgan
Lt. Scott Morgan
Kurt von Rachen
Barry Randolph
Capt. Humbert Reynolds

list included: Rene Lafayette, Captain Charles Gordon, Lt. Scott Morgan and the notorious Kurt von Rachen—supposedly on the lam for a murder rap, while hammering out two-fisted prose in Argentina. The point: While L. Ron Hubbard as Ken Martin spun stories of Southeast Asian intrigue, LRH as Barry Randolph authored tales of romance on the Western range—which, stretching between a dozen genres is how he came to stand among the two hundred elite authors providing close to a million tales through the glory days of American Pulp Fiction.

L. Ron Hubbard, circa 1930, at the outset of a literary career that would finally span half a century.

In evidence of exactly that, by 1936 L. Ron Hubbard was literally leading pulp fiction's elite as president of New York's American Fiction Guild. Members included a veritable pulp hall of fame: Lester "Doc Savage" Dent, Walter "The Shadow" Gibson, and the legendary Dashiell Hammett—to cite but a few.

Also in evidence of just where L. Ron Hubbard stood within his first two years on the American pulp circuit: By the spring of 1937, he was ensconced in Hollywood, adopting a Caribbean thriller for Columbia Pictures, remembered today as *The Secret of Treasure Island.* Comprising fifteen thirty-minute episodes, the L. Ron Hubbard screenplay led to the most profitable matinée serial in Hollywood history. In accord with Hollywood culture, he was thereafter continually called upon

The 1937 Secret of Treasure Island, *a fifteen-episode serial adapted for the screen by L. Ron Hubbard from his novel,* Murder at Pirate Castle.

to rewrite/doctor scripts—most famously for long-time friend and fellow adventurer Clark Gable.

In the interim—and herein lies another distinctive chapter of the L. Ron Hubbard story—he continually worked to open Pulp Kingdom gates to up-and-coming authors. Or, for that matter, anyone who wished to write. It was a fairly unconventional stance, as markets were already thin and competition razor sharp. But the fact remains, it was an L. Ron Hubbard hallmark that he vehemently lobbied on behalf of young authors—regularly supplying instructional articles to trade journals, guest-lecturing to short story classes at George Washington University and Harvard, and even founding his own creative writing competition. It was established in 1940, dubbed the Golden Pen, and guaranteed winners both New York representation and publication in *Argosy*.

But it was John W. Campbell Jr.'s *Astounding Science Fiction* that finally proved the most memorable LRH vehicle. While every fan of L. Ron Hubbard's galactic epics undoubtedly knows the story, it nonetheless bears repeating: By late 1938, the pulp publishing magnate of Street & Smith was determined to revamp *Astounding Science Fiction* for broader readership. In particular, senior editorial director F. Orlin Tremaine called for stories with a stronger *human element*. When acting editor John W. Campbell balked, preferring his spaceship-driven tales, Tremaine enlisted Hubbard. Hubbard, in turn, replied with the genre's first truly *character-driven* works, wherein heroes are pitted not against bug-eyed monsters but the mystery and majesty of deep space itself—and thus was launched the Golden Age of Science Fiction.

The names alone are enough to quicken the pulse of any science fiction aficionado, including LRH friend and protégé, Robert Heinlein, Isaac Asimov, A. E. van Vogt and Ray Bradbury. Moreover, when coupled with LRH stories of fantasy, we further come to what's rightly been described as the foundation of every modern tale of horror: L. Ron Hubbard's immortal *Fear.* It was rightly proclaimed by Stephen King as one of the very few works to genuinely warrant that overworked term "classic"—as in: *"This is a classic tale of creeping, surreal menace and horror. . . . This is one of the really, really good ones."*

L. Ron Hubbard, 1948, among fellow science fiction luminaries at the World Science Fiction Convention in Toronto.

To accommodate the greater body of L. Ron Hubbard fantasies, Street & Smith inaugurated *Unknown*—a classic pulp if there ever was one, and wherein readers were soon thrilling to the likes of *Typewriter in the Sky* and *Slaves of Sleep* of which Frederik Pohl would declare: *"There are bits and pieces from Ron's work that became part of the language in ways that very few other writers managed."*

And, indeed, at J. W. Campbell Jr.'s insistence, Ron was regularly drawing on themes from the Arabian Nights and so introducing readers to a world of genies, jinn, Aladdin and Sinbad—all of which, of course, continue to float through cultural mythology to this day.

At least as influential in terms of post-apocalypse stories was L. Ron Hubbard's 1940 *Final Blackout*. Generally acclaimed as the finest anti-war novel of the decade and among the ten best works of the genre ever authored—here, too, was a tale that would live on in ways few other writers imagined.

Portland, Oregon, 1943; L. Ron Hubbard, captain of the US Navy subchaser PC 815.

Hence, the later Robert Heinlein verdict: "Final Blackout *is as perfect a piece of science fiction as has ever been written.*"

Like many another who both lived and wrote American pulp adventure, the war proved a tragic end to Ron's sojourn in the pulps. He served with distinction in four theaters and was highly decorated for commanding corvettes in the North Pacific. He was also grievously wounded in combat, lost many a close friend and colleague and thus resolved to say farewell to pulp fiction and devote himself to what it had supported these many years—namely, his serious research.

But in no way was the LRH literary saga at an end, for as he wrote some thirty years later, in 1980:

"Recently there came a period when I had little to do. This was novel in a life so crammed with busy years, and I decided to amuse myself by writing a novel that was pure science fiction."

That work was *Battlefield Earth: A Saga of the Year 3000*. It was an immediate *New York Times* bestseller and, in fact, the first international science fiction blockbuster in decades. It was not, however, L. Ron Hubbard's magnum opus, as that distinction is generally reserved for his next and final work: The 1.2 million word *Mission Earth*.

> **Final Blackout**
> *is as perfect a piece of science fiction as has ever been written.*
>
> —Robert Heinlein

How he managed those 1.2 million words in just over twelve months is yet another piece of the L. Ron Hubbard legend. But the fact remains, he did indeed author a ten-volume *dekalogy* that lives in publishing history for the fact that each and every volume of the series was also a *New York Times* bestseller.

Moreover, as subsequent generations discovered L. Ron Hubbard through republished works and novelizations of his screenplays, the mere fact of his name on a cover signaled an international bestseller. . . . Until, to date, sales of his works exceed hundreds of millions, and he otherwise remains among the most enduring and widely read authors in literary history. Although as a final word on the tales of L. Ron Hubbard, perhaps it's enough to simply reiterate what editors told readers in the glory days of American Pulp Fiction:

He writes the way he does, brothers, because he's been there, seen it and done it!

THE STORIES FROM THE GOLDEN AGE

Your ticket to adventure starts here with the Stories from
the Golden Age collection by master storyteller L. Ron Hubbard.
These gripping tales are set in a kaleidoscope of exotic locales and brim
with fascinating characters, including some of the
most vile villains, dangerous dames and brazen heroes
you'll ever get to meet.

The entire collection of over one hundred and fifty stories is being
released in a series of eighty books and audiobooks.
For an up-to-date listing of available titles,
go to www.goldenagestories.com.

AIR ADVENTURE

Arctic Wings	*Man-Killers of the Air*
The Battling Pilot	*On Blazing Wings*
Boomerang Bomber	*Red Death Over China*
The Crate Killer	*Sabotage in the Sky*
The Dive Bomber	*Sky Birds Dare!*
Forbidden Gold	*The Sky-Crasher*
Hurtling Wings	*Trouble on His Wings*
The Lieutenant Takes the Sky	*Wings Over Ethiopia*

FAR-FLUNG ADVENTURE

SEA ADVENTURE

TALES FROM THE ORIENT

MYSTERY

FANTASY

SCIENCE FICTION

WESTERN